In Darkness,
DEATH

IN DARKNESS,
DEATH

DOROTHY
and
THOMAS
HOOBLER

PHILOMEL BOOKS / NEW YORK

Library of Congress Cataloging-in-Publication Data
Hoobler, Dorothy.
In darkness, death / Dorothy and Thomas Hoobler.
p. cm. Sequel to: The demon in the teahouse.
Summary: In eighteenth-century Japan, young Seikei becomes involved with a
ninja as he helps Judge Ooka, his foster father, investigate the murder of a samurai.
1. Japan—History—Tokugawa period, 1600–1868—Juvenile fiction.
[1. Japan—History—Tokugawa period, 1600–1868—Fiction.
2. Samurai—Fiction. 3. Ninja—Fiction. 4. Ooka, Tadasuke, 1677?–1751?—
Fiction. 5. Mystery and detective stories.] I. Hoobler, Thomas. II. Title.
PZ7.H76227Ni 2004 [Fic]—dc21 2003005383 ISBN 0-399-23767-4

First Impression 10 9 8 7 6 5 4 3 2 1

To our daughter, Ellen.

Contents

In Darkness,
DEATH

1 —
In Darkness, Death

It was the hour of the rat; throughout the castle only shadows moved. As the moon made its lonely journey across the night sky, dark shapes slid across floors and walls, one step ahead of the light.

And when one black form, quicker than the other shadows, slithered down a hallway, no guard sounded a challenge.

Earlier that night, many guests had arrived for Lord Inaba's party, and extra servants had been hired. No one had paid particular attention to a round-bellied wine steward who was somewhat clumsy, but seemed eager to please. He neglected no one in his efforts to keep the sake cups filled, even pressing Lord Inaba's bodyguards to drink a little, though certainly not enough to affect their alertness.

Now, however, the powder that the steward had slipped into the sake had had enough time to take effect. Guards, guests, servants, family, and Lord Inaba himself all lay as peacefully unaware as the dead.

All except the shadow. Anyone who had been awake to see would have been surprised at how much more gracefully the round-bellied wine steward moved now.

As he moved into the corridor that led to Lord Inaba's room, the floor sang. The shadow paid no attention, for no one but he could hear. Two samurai *guards sat on the floor in front of Lord Inaba's door, their heads slumped down on their chests. The shadow touched each of them in turn and whispered into their ears. Then he stepped between them and drew a short sword from beneath his plain* kimono. *Men like Lord Inaba had enemies; his door would be barred to prevent entry. So the shadow pierced the decorated paper that covered the door frame, drawing his sword down it with no more noise than a falcon makes descending on its prey.*

He stepped nimbly through the sliced paper. The daimyo *lord, lying on a large, thickly padded mat, did not stir. He had drunk many cups of sake that night as his guests toasted his return to Edo.*

The shadow wasted no time in carrying out his task. In a moment, the smell of death was in the room. Wiping his blade on a corner of the sleeping mat, the shadow said a silent prayer to ward off Lord Inaba's angry spirit.

The shadow untied his garment then, showing the source of his fat belly. Unwrapping coils of rope from around his waist, he stood, thinner now, to tie one end to a lantern hook on the wall. He lowered the rest of the rope out the window.

Climbing onto the windowsill, he looked back inside the room, now polluted by death. He shook his sleeve and something fluttered out, landing on the floor near the widening pool of blood. And then he was gone.

Seikei wrinkled his nose. The coppery odor in the room brought back a disturbing memory. He had smelled it before when he had witnessed the death of the *kabuki* actor Tomomi. Of course, Tomomi had welcomed his death—had in fact led Seikei on a long, carefully prepared journey to see it.

This death—the one that had taken place in this room—was different. Lord Inaba had not gone to sleep thinking that his throat would be slit in the night. He had guards throughout his castle to protect him from all harm. For some reason, none of them had stopped the assassin from entering the room—in fact, no one had even seen him.

That much Seikei had learned from his foster father, Judge Ooka. Early that morning, the judge had awakened Seikei. "I have a mission to perform," he said. That was all Seikei needed to know. He rose and dressed at once. The judge would not have awakened him unless he wanted Seikei to go along.

And indeed, when Seikei went outside, he saw two horses already saddled and waiting. Seikei mounted his, pleased that he could now do so without needing a boost from Bunzo, the judge's devoted samurai retainer, who had been assigned the unenviable task of teaching Seikei the skills a samurai should possess.

Seikei had never learned those skills before now,

because he had unluckily been born the son of a wealthy merchant. No matter how prosperous, merchants were the lowest members of society—below artisans and craftsworkers, farmers, and of course, samurai warriors, who stood highest of all. Thus, it seemed to be Seikei's destiny to remain a merchant, for each person must accept the place his ancestors occupied.

But when Seikei had shown courage in helping to solve the mystery of the theft of a valuable jewel from an inn on the Tokaido Road, Judge Ooka had adopted him as his own son. It was a great honor to be accepted into a samurai family, and Seikei tried to be worthy of it.

Sometimes he felt he was not succeeding. He doubted he could ever shoot an arrow as well as Bunzo or the judge, although on the few occasions Seikei had battled an opponent with a sword, he had not done badly. He could write verses well enough, but he found other samurai arts difficult, especially flower arranging.

Seikei's horsemanship had improved lately, somewhat earning him Bunzo's respect. "You know," Bunzo had told him yesterday, "I once thought we could lose you merely by putting you on the back of a strong horse. But now I see we will have to find some other way."

As the judge emerged from the house and mounted his horse—more nimbly than anyone seeing his round, heavy figure would have suspected—his housekeeper,

Noka, followed. She carried a black lacquer *bento* box. Seikei knew what was inside: food for the journey. As she handed it to him, he felt embarrassed.

"Isn't there one for the judge?" Seikei asked.

"He had his breakfast already," said Noka. "But you're going all the way to Edo, and I knew you'd be hungry."

Seikei thanked her politely, glancing at the judge, who was trying to hide a smile. Noka treated Seikei as if he were a child. A samurai should be willing to go for days without food, train himself to endure any hardship in the service of his lord.

The judge knew just what Seikei was thinking. "If there is too much food in that box for you," he said, "I will be glad to help you finish it."

Seikei handed him the box, secretly hoping the judge wouldn't eat it all. They set off then, letting the horses go at their own pace, for the ground was frozen and covered with a thin layer of snow. It would take them most of the morning to travel from their home in the countryside to Edo, the city from which the *shogun* governed all of Japan. He often called on the judge to solve problems that no one else could. Recently the judge had organized a system of fire brigades to protect the city against the huge blazes that in the past had burned out of control for days.

The judge's chief duty, of course, was to help keep order by arresting criminals and determining the proper punishment for them. On more than one occasion, he had used Seikei to gather information for him. Seikei hoped this would be one of those times.

After returning the bento box to Seikei—there were still a few tasty pieces of eel and some rice in it—the judge started to explain. "A messenger from the shogun arrived very early this morning. Yesterday, Lord Inaba was slain by an assassin while he lay sleeping in his residence in Edo."

Seikei nearly gasped. Lord Inaba was one of the most powerful daimyos, or lords, in the country. For an assassin to be able to get close to him was almost unthinkable. Seikei had many questions, but he knew better than to interrupt the judge.

"Of course," the judge continued, "this would be a serious matter at any time, but it is particularly grave because Lord Inaba had just arrived in Edo for his required visit. Thus, he was under the protection of the shogun. His death is a personal embarrassment to the shogun, and the fact that the assassin has escaped only makes it worse."

Seikei understood. To prevent any of the powerful daimyos from plotting to overthrow him, the shogun required them to spend one year out of every two in Edo, where he could closely watch their activities. The rule was popular with the city's merchants, who gained rich customers forced to buy from them. However, it meant that the shogun had to guarantee the safety of the daimyos, their families, and the samurai who served them. If a daimyo—or any member of his household—were harmed while living in Edo, the shogun would be disgraced, unless he avenged the crime. That was the only way to preserve his honor, and as Seikei knew, to a samurai honor was more important than life itself.

Seikei waited for the judge to provide more details about the assassination, but for a time they rode in silence, except for the sound of the horses' hooves. Snow began to fall, and Seikei imagined the two of them riding through a scene in a colorful print, like the ones he had seen for sale in Edo.

Finally the judge remarked, "It is too bad that we could not examine the scene earlier. Lord Inaba was killed while he slept. By now his servants will have removed the body. That is unfortunate."

Seikei knew that the judge's reputation as a brilliant investigator was well earned. People said he could tell a criminal just by looking at him. The judge once told Seikei that this wasn't true, but because people believed it, some criminals confessed as soon as they were brought into the judge's presence.

The judge had taught Seikei that the best method of catching a criminal was to notice things carefully and think about what they meant. "A criminal disturbs the proper order of things," he said, "like a stone that falls into a pond. If you follow the circles that ripple through the water, you will come back to the stone."

That was a simple explanation, but Seikei found that it was harder to do than it sounded. The judge had occasionally sent him to look for information that would help solve a crime, but Seikei had trouble determining what was useful and what was not.

When they arrived at Lord Inaba's castle, they saw that it was now guarded by samurai who wore garments decorated with hollyhocks—the symbol of the Tokugawa family, whose members had held the post of shogun for more than a century. Seikei wondered where Lord Inaba's own guards had gone.

He soon found out. After the shogun's guards let them enter the castle, an angry young samurai greeted them. *Greeted* was not the right word, for he displayed a profound lack of politeness. "Are you the judge who is supposed to find the criminal who did this?" he asked abruptly, without introducing himself. "You've taken your time getting here. I have sent three messengers to the shogun and received nothing but excuses."

The judge bowed as if he hadn't noticed the man's rudeness. "I am Ooka," he said, "a judge in the service of the shogun. I extend the shogun's sincere regret at the death of Lord Inaba, your father."

The young man seemed a little surprised at being addressed in such a manner. He bowed in return—although still too abruptly, Seikei noticed—and said, "I am Yutaro, eldest son of the family Inaba."

"May we see the room where your father was struck down?" asked the judge.

"It is still unclean," replied Yutaro. "The priests have not yet come to perform the purification rites."

The judge nodded. Seikei knew that was good news to him. "We will risk it," he said.

As Yutaro led them up a flight of stairs, the judge asked, "Did your father have any enemies?"

"None at all," Yutaro answered quickly—too quickly to have thought about the question, it seemed to Seikei. "This is the work of a thief, and the lazy guards are to blame. They claim they saw nothing."

"I would like to question them," said the judge.

Yutaro shrugged. "I ordered the shogun's men to take them away, for who could trust such bunglers? Perhaps they have been executed by now."

The judge paused. "Do you suspect the guards of deliberately betraying your father?"

Waving his hand, Yutaro said, "What does it matter? They failed in their duty. The reason does not concern me."

They walked up several flights of stairs to reach Lord Inaba's room. It was on the top floor of the imposing castle. "Do you sleep here too?" asked the judge.

"No," said Yutaro. "My father reserved this part of the castle for himself alone. My mother is dead."

As they began to walk down the corridor toward the

room where Lord Inaba had been killed, the floorboards squeaked loudly—so loudly that Seikei took a step back. "This is a nightingale floor," the judge explained. "The wooden planks are set in such a way that they 'sing' whenever someone steps on them. It is meant to alert the guards that someone is approaching."

"Little good it did," said Yutaro angrily.

"Where were the guards?" asked the judge when they reached the door where the paper had been slit.

"Two of them were stationed directly in front of this door," replied Yutaro.

"So they could not have failed to see an intruder," the judge said.

"Certainly not," said Yutaro, the rude tone creeping into his voice again.

"How could they have missed seeing someone enter?" the judge asked, turning to Seikei.

Seikei knew that the judge wanted him to think of an answer. "Maybe they left their posts," Seikei said, "to investigate a disturbance somewhere else."

The judge nodded. "Or?"

"They might have been asleep," Seikei suggested. Although they would have had to be sleeping very deeply, he thought.

"Both of them?" Yutaro asked sarcastically.

The judge waved his hand to encourage Seikei to keep thinking. "Anything else?"

Seikei frowned. The judge must see something he

did not. What could it be? Then it came to him. It didn't seem possible, but the judge had once told him, "When we do not know the answer, we must consider all possibilities, no matter how unlikely."

"Well," said Seikei, "he could have been invisible."

Yutaro snorted with contempt. Seikei's face felt hot. The judge merely smiled and said, "That is, indeed, a possibility."

He slid open the door. "Let us look further," he said.

Yutaro did not follow them, but stood outside in the corridor, listening.

The body had been removed, but the coppery blood scent lingered like faint incense. A dark stain on the floor stopped at the place where the sleeping mat had lain. That too was gone, probably to be burned. The blood itself would not be cleaned up until Shinto priests came to drive away the bad *kami*, or spirits.

The judge pointed to the rope that led from the lantern hook to the window. "At least we know how the assassin escaped. He did not fly away."

Seikei wondered whether the judge was teasing him about his earlier suggestion. As if to reassure him, the judge went on: "But he could have been invisible, if he were a *ninja*."

A ninja? When Seikei and his brothers had been very young, their mother used to frighten them when they misbehaved by telling them stories of the ninjas. They could come and go wherever they wished, because they had magic powers that they could use to make themselves invisible. They came in the night to capture naughty children while they slept and punished them in ways too horrible to be described.

"Are there really such people as ninjas?" Seikei asked.

"Yes, most certainly there are," replied the judge. "Look at this rope. It's made of silk. Just the sort of thing a ninja would use. Light enough to be carried easily, but strong enough to hold—come see."

Seikei joined the judge at the window and looked down. He felt dizzy at the thought of falling. "You see," the judge said, "the assassin would not have needed to put his full weight on the rope. He could have balanced his feet against the wall on the way down. Still, he could not have weighed as much as I do."

The judge gave Seikei a glance. Seikei's stomach churned as he realized the judge might ask him to test the rope by climbing down it.

Instead, the judge whispered, as if he didn't want Yutaro to hear from the corridor, "Have you noticed anything else that provides us with a clue to the assassin's identity?"

Seikei examined the rope carefully. It was made of black silk. The knot that held it to the lantern hook was not unusual, just a secure knot of the kind anyone would use.

He looked around the room. Had the assassin left

any other trace of himself? Not the weapon he must have used to slit the daimyo's throat. Seikei trained his eyes on the spot where the judge was looking.

There was an outline on the floor traced by the dried blood. Something had been there earlier when the blood had flowed around it. Seikei bent to study its shape. "A wing?" he said, puzzled.

"We must talk to the servants who cleared the room," said the judge.

THE BUTTERFLY

There is a disadvantage to being feared," the judge had once told Seikei. "People sometimes confess to crimes they did not commit."

"Why would anyone do that?" asked Seikei.

"They want to avoid being tortured."

"But *you* don't use torture to get people to confess," Seikei said. The judge had often said that such methods were useless in finding the truth.

"Unfortunately," replied the judge, "they know that I can, if I wish."

It was apparent from the looks of the servants that they were thinking of torture, if not something worse. Yutaro, Lord Inaba's son, had done nothing to reassure them. After the judge asked to question the servants, Yutaro brought them together like a flock of chickens. They assembled in a room downstairs where there was a shrine to a Buddhist saint, with a candle burning in front of it. The servants huddled together as closely as possible, and when they saw the judge, with the two swords under his belt marking him as a samurai, they all dropped to their hands and knees, tangling their legs together in their haste.

Seikei saw that there were seven of them: five women and two men. "Look up, if you please," the judge told them. Reluctantly their eyes rose from the floor.

"Which of you removed Lord Inaba's body from his room?" the judge asked.

"We were ordered to do it," protested one of the men in a shrill voice. The other man nodded vigorously.

"I understand," said the judge quietly. "When was this?"

"Yesterday morning, after they found him dead," the man said.

"What is your name?" asked the judge.

The man looked around as if he were sorry he'd spoken. He bowed his head and murmured, "Doppo."

"Who was it who found Lord Inaba?" asked the judge.

"One of the guards. It was their fault. We were all in our rooms asleep."

The others nodded, some of them murmuring agreement.

"Did anyone besides the guards enter the room before you moved the body?"

The two men looked at each other, and Doppo finally spoke. "Just Yutaro. I mean . . . Lord Inaba."

The judge paused before saying, "The new Lord Inaba."

"Yes. He is our lord now." Doppo glanced at Yutaro, who was standing to one side of the room. Seikei thought Yutaro seemed pleased that the servant referred to him that way, and of course that was just what Doppo had hoped to see.

"*Did* you enter the room while the body was there?" the judge asked, directing his question at Yutaro. Seikei could see that the new Lord Inaba did not like being questioned in the same manner as his servants. But of course the judge represented the shogun, and could in theory torture anyone to obtain a response. . . .

Even so, it took Yutaro a moment to answer. Seikei could see he was trying to think what the best reply would be, instead of what the truth was. "I did," he said finally.

The judge looked back at Doppo. "Did you see anything on the floor when you removed the body?" he asked.

Doppo furrowed his brows. "The lord was on the floor."

"He was on a mat," corrected the judge.

Doppo looked as if he'd been tricked. "Well, then, the mat was on the floor. I noticed *that*."

The judge glanced around at the others. "The mat has also been removed. Who took it?"

"We were *ordered* to," said one of the women.

"Yes, yes," the judge said impatiently. "I understand that. What is your name?"

"Shiwo." She was middle-aged and looked as if she had some authority in the household. Without being prompted, she went on: "We took the mat and burned it, for it was impure with the lord's blood."

"And the blood on the floor . . . ," the judge began.

"We were waiting for the Shinto priest before we cleaned that up," said Shiwo. "But you showed up first."

"So I did. When you took the mat away, did you notice anything else on the floor?"

"Just the blood, as your lordship said."

"You said *we* took the mat. Who else was with you?"

"No one, Lord. Only Hana." Shiwo gestured to a girl about twelve years old next to her. "She's a little slow," Shiwo said with a wink at the judge. "Doesn't know anything *you* might want to know."

At the mention of her name, Hana looked terrified. Her eyes, pinned on the judge, couldn't have been any wider if she had been watching a dragon.

The judge gave her a glance, thought for a moment, and then announced, "I would like everyone to come upstairs and show me exactly what you did in the room." He paused. "Except Hana. You may stay here."

Taking Seikei by the arm, the judge spoke softly in his ear: "I want you to question Hana. She may have picked up whatever was on the floor. I need to know what it was."

Seikei wanted to ask the judge how he should draw this information from a girl who looked too frightened to speak. But he realized he was supposed to find that out on his own.

When the others had left, the girl knelt in a corner of the room as if she hoped Seikei wouldn't notice her. He went a little closer. "What kind of work do you do?" he asked.

She looked as if she couldn't believe he was speaking to her. As he held her gaze, however, she said softly, "Whatever anybody wants. Shiwo's in charge of us. She tells me what to do."

"And she told you to help her remove the mat from Lord Inaba's room?"

"Yes. I was scared. I would never have dared to go there otherwise."

"I believe you," Seikei said. Hana didn't seem to be the courageous type.

"And I wouldn't have taken anything if I'd thought it was valuable," she added.

"Um . . . you wouldn't?"

Hana put her hand over her mouth as if she realized she had said too much.

"Well, it probably wasn't valuable," said Seikei.

"I didn't think it was," Hana replied. "And anyway, it

was spoiled. Nobody would want it, that's what *I* thought. Nobody would even miss it. Shiwo would just have burned it if she'd seen it."

Seikei tried to figure out how to get her to tell him just what *it* was. "Yes," he said, "but the judge noticed. Nothing escapes him."

The girl was silent for a moment. Then a tear fell from her eye, cascading down her cheek. Then one from the other eye, followed by another, and another.

Seikei was as alarmed as if she had sprung a leak and would soon engulf the room in tears. "Stop that!" he said.

She hung her head so he couldn't see her crying. "If any of us are caught stealing," she said between sobs, "we're immediately dismissed. And I have no place to go. My parents are dead, and my grandmother said I was very lucky to find a place in Lord Inaba's household. She's probably dead too."

After a little while, she quieted down. "Are you finished crying?" Seikei asked.

She shook her head no.

"Look, I have an idea," he said. "Give me what you picked up in the room, and I won't tell anyone."

She gave Seikei a look of surprise. The tears on her cheeks still distressed him, but he tried to appear calm.

"You won't?" she asked. "Truly?"

"Well, I have to tell the judge," he said, "but—"

He stopped because she had started to cry again. "He will punish me, I know," she sniffled.

"No, don't worry," said Seikei. "He's really very kind. I know he'll forgive you."

She looked into his eyes. "You swear?" she asked.

"On my honor as a samurai," he said, putting his hand on the wooden sword he carried under his *obi*.

Abruptly she threw her arms around his knees. He looked around, fearing that someone would enter the room and see. "Let go, now," he said. "If you don't give me the thing before the judge returns, he may not forgive you."

"Oh," she said. She released him and reached inside her kimono. Drawing something out, she opened her hand to reveal a butterfly.

It was made of folded paper, crumpled now and partly stained with dark blood. But unmistakably it had been intended as a butterfly, for the red paper wings were painted with black spots, just like a real butterfly.

"I didn't think anybody would want it," Hana said in a small voice.

"It could help us find the person who killed Lord Inaba," said Seikei.

Hana smiled as if she knew Seikei was trying to fool her. "Oh, you'll never find *him*," she said.

"Why not?"

"Because it was a ninja. That's what the servants all say."

"How do they know? Did anyone see him?"

"Of course not. You can't see ninjas. That's how they *know* it was a ninja."

Seikei couldn't think of an answer to this, but he reminded himself that all possibilities must be considered.

"Why would a ninja want to kill Lord Inaba?" he asked.

Hana shrugged. "Somebody must have paid him."

"Who would do that?"

"I don't know. You're the judge's assistant, aren't you?"

Seikei was annoyed at himself. The judge had often told him, "Never let people you are questioning ask *you* the questions." Before he could reply, however, the judge returned. He was by himself and gave Seikei a questioning look. Seikei held up the butterfly.

"Very good," said the judge. He turned to Hana. "Thank you for saving this for us."

"I . . . I didn't think—" she began.

"This didn't belong to Lord Inaba, did it?" asked the judge.

"Oh, no." Hana seemed horrified by the thought. "I would never take anything that belonged to the lord."

"Just so," said the judge. "You may go now."

She lost no time doing that, scrambling to her feet and backing out the doorway while bowing many times at the judge. Seikei thought he himself received a grateful glance just before she disappeared.

The judge took the paper butterfly from Seikei and turned it over in his hands.

"What does it mean?" said Seikei.

"It tells us who the assassin is," replied the judge.

3 —
THE TRAIL
BEGINS HERE

Seikei stared. Though he knew Judge Ooka had great powers of deduction, he could hardly believe the judge had solved the case simply by looking at a paper butterfly.

The judge saw Seikei's confusion, and smiled. "There is still much work to do before we apprehend the assassin," he said.

"But who is he?" asked Seikei.

"And, of course, I do not yet know his name," said the judge. "But as you know, once we understand a person's actions and motives, finding him is no more difficult than following the tracks of a deer in the forest. If we continue with persistence, eventually the deer will stop to rest and we will catch him."

Seikei thought it would be harder than that. "How did the butterfly tell you all this?"

"Actually, the butterfly has even more secrets to tell us. But I was asking other questions while you were finding the butterfly. Since you were not present, I will explain."

He stopped because Shiwo had appeared at the doorway. "Would your lordship care for something to eat?" she asked.

"That would be most welcome," said the judge. "Can you bring trays to us here?"

"Whatever you wish," she replied.

After she left, the judge told Seikei, "Pay attention to the quality of the food we are served."

Seikei wondered if the judge were letting his love of food overshadow his interest in capturing the criminal. Immediately Seikei chided himself for thinking such a disloyal thought.

Again the judge smiled, and Seikei hung his head as if his foster father could indeed read his thoughts.

"Do you recall," the judge asked, "when the new Lord Inaba—Yutaro—said he thought the assassin was a thief?"

"Yes," Seikei said, glad that he had paid attention earlier.

"Upstairs, I asked him and the servants what had been stolen. They could not answer—that is, they could find nothing that was missing. The young lord suggested that the thief was frightened away before he could steal anything. Do you believe that?"

Seikei thought rapidly. "Everyone was asleep. No one ever saw the assassin. He could not have been frightened away."

"So it was," said the judge. "And what else did Yutaro tell us that we must now reject?"

This was a more difficult question. Seikei thought over what he remembered Yutaro saying. Then it came to him: "That his father, the old Lord Inaba, had no enemies."

The pleased look on the judge's face was Seikei's greatest reward. "Just so," said the judge.

Shiwo appeared then, carrying a tray of food for the two of them. When she set it down, Seikei saw that it held only two small bowls of plain rice and a dish of seaweed with a little soy sauce sprinkled over it. There were also two cups of tea. Seikei's family had been tea merchants for five generations, and he could smell without tasting it that it was inferior tea. To be served such a meager meal in a lord's castle was almost insulting.

Then Seikei realized that was what the judge had told him to notice.

The judge made no comment on the food. He merely picked up his chopsticks and began to eat.

When Shiwo had departed, however, Seikei asked, "Why are we being served this kind of food?"

"Ordinarily," said the judge, "I would take it to mean we are not welcome here."

Seikei finished his bowl of rice quickly, since he hadn't eaten much for breakfast. It took an effort for him to leave most of the seaweed for the judge.

After the judge put down the empty bowl, he folded his hands on his belly and closed his eyes. A look of satisfaction slowly crept over his face, as if he had just enjoyed a magnificent feast.

Seikei knew there was nothing to do but wait. Bunzo had taught him that if you wanted time to pass quickly, it helped to concentrate on a sound. Seikei thought of a time when he had heard the *geisha* Umae singing. Just at the point where her voice was highest in a lovely melody . . .

But his mind kept wandering to other things. The butterfly. How did it tell the judge who the assassin was? Who was he, anyway? An enemy of Lord Inaba's? What did the meal they'd been served have to do with—

"I am thinking," the judge said unexpectedly, his eyes still closed, "of a wonderful meal I once had at the house of a man who loved food as much as I do. Have you ever tasted *soba* noodles with whipped mountain yam and quail eggs?"

"No," answered Seikei.

"A pity. Then you would have something to think about after a meal like this one."

"You said the meal means we aren't welcome here," said Seikei. "Does that mean we should leave?"

"Not yet," replied the judge. "I want to see how unwelcome we are." He seemed to relax again, and Seikei knew there was more waiting to be done.

Seikei closed his eyes and tried to think of a meal *he*

had particularly liked. It didn't take him long. *Okayu*—rice porridge that his mother had often fixed. Eating okayu had always made Seikei feel secure, as if nothing bad could ever happen. But of course, bad things did happen. Life with his old father had not been easy.

His father—the one Seikei had been born with—had always told Seikei how foolish he was. "Wishing to be a samurai—you know that is impossible! And even if it *were* possible, you would not like it!"

Father meant that the life of a samurai was much harder than that of a tea merchant. He was right—that was why merchants were so looked down upon. Father did not see the point of practicing the many things a samurai must be skilled at—besides archery, swordsmanship, and hand-to-hand combat, a samurai should know how to write poetry, arrange flowers in an artistic fashion, and even conduct a formal tea ceremony. Except for the tea ceremony, Father couldn't see how any of those skills helped you make money.

Seikei found all those things difficult, it was true. (Except for writing poetry, which he had always done whenever Father did not notice.) Sometimes, he thought he would never master them. He had not even earned the right to carry the two steel swords—one long, one short—that only a samurai could wear. For now, he had to be content with the wooden one. But as the judge had told him, "If your heart is that of a samurai, a wooden sword is as mighty as a steel one."

The door to the room opened, and Yutaro stood there. "Have you seen everything you need to see?" he asked.

The judge opened his eyes slowly, as if Yutaro had awakened him from a nap. "I have seen the assassin," he said.

Yutaro looked stunned. He glanced around the room. "Where is he? Has he come back?"

"I should have said, I have seen what the assassin is like," replied the judge. "It's nearly the same thing."

Yutaro's face clouded. "I expect more than that," he said. "The shogun told me he was sending the best investigator he had. If that is true, it is surprising anyone in Edo considers themselves safe."

The judge bowed his head. "We will try to do a little better," he said. Turning to Seikei, he added, "*Now* is the time for us to leave."

Yutaro escorted them to the castle entrance. Seikei's ears were burning. He could not understand why the judge allowed himself to be insulted in such a manner. Seikei could hardly restrain himself from drawing his wooden sword. It would be strong enough to break open Yutaro's skull.

Outside, the judge said to Seikei, "You are learning to control yourself, I see. But I could still feel your anger, and I suspect Yutaro could too."

"Weren't you angry?" Seikei asked.

"Should I have been?"

"Yutaro insulted you."

"That was his intention, clearly. In my youth, I would have been tempted to draw my sword and see which of us was more skillful. After that, almost certainly one of us would have died."

"I am sure you would not have been the loser."

"Possibly. It is unwise to assume that just because someone has no manners, he is an inferior swordsman as well. In any case, if I defeated him, then I would have to report to the shogun that I carried out his order to find the assassin of Lord Inaba by killing his son, the new Lord Inaba." The judge glanced at Seikei. "What do you think the shogun would ask me to do then?"

Seikei didn't want to answer, but he had to. "He would expect you to commit *seppuku,* to kill yourself."

"And I would be grateful, because he would be saving me from the disgrace of doing anything that foolish again."

"But still," Seikei protested. "Your honor as a samurai—"

"If you think your honor demands that you kill every dog who barks at you," said the judge, cutting him off, "you will only find yourself spending all your time chasing dogs. There is no honor in that."

The judge led Seikei around to the side of Lord Inaba's castle. He pointed to the window high above, from which the assassin had lowered himself. "It took a courageous man to climb down from that height," said the judge. "It would be an honorable achievement to capture him."

Seikei looked around the snow-covered ground. Only a few animal tracks were visible. The judge pointed to them. "Those are the marks a fox would make," he said.

"Yes," Seikei agreed. "The snow must have continued to fall and covered up the murderer's footprints."

"Perhaps," said the judge. "Let us go see the guards who let him into Lord Inaba's room."

They mounted their horses and rode toward the shogun's palace. The ride was slow because the city's streets, as always, were crowded. Samurai whose wraparound *kosodes* were marked with the crests of the daimyos they served swaggered through the street, each one ready to assert the greatness of his lord above all others. There would have been continual bloody fights in the capital's roadways had it not been that the shogun banned all combat inside the city. The penalty for violating the order was death.

Several times, passing samurai glanced furtively at the judge. The chrysanthemum crest on his kosode, of course, marked him as one of the shogun's officials, but his size was an indication to many that he was the famous Judge Ooka. A few samurai even greeted him with a bow of respect, and shopkeepers who were in the doorways trying to attract customers bowed very low as he passed. Although none of these people paid any attention to Seikei, he took pride in the respect shown to his foster father.

Suddenly Judge Ooka reined in his horse. *"Hai!"* he shouted. "Tatsuno!" Seikei looked in the direction the judge was facing. The only person he saw was a thin, shabby-looking man in a plain brown kimono. As soon as the man heard the judge shout, he turned and slipped down an alley between two shops.

"Go after him," the judge told Seikei. "I want to talk to him."

4 —
CAPTURING A NINJA

Seikei urged his horse toward the alley where the thin man had disappeared. He soon saw, however, that it was too narrow for the horse to go inside, so he dismounted and ran on foot.

It was dark inside the alley. The shopkeepers on either side had built a roof over it to protect the goods stored there. Dimly, Seikei could see wicker baskets and wooden crates stacked along the walls—but no thin man.

He must be hiding behind one of the crates, Seikei realized. With one hand on the hilt of his wooden sword, he made his way carefully from one crate to another. The thin man had not been wearing a sword, but he might be carrying some other kind of weapon.

Without warning, Seikei caught sight of a swift movement farther up the alley. He looked just in time to see the back of a brown kimono. "Stop!" he shouted, and ran after it.

The thin man disappeared again, just as swiftly as

before. But Seikei kept running, sure that his quarry was somewhere up ahead.

Suddenly he felt a stabbing pain in the bottom of one of his feet. As he put the other foot down, the same pain shot upward through his other foot. Involuntarily, he hopped about, trying to get away from whatever was causing the pain.

Finally he fell down—fortunately falling backwards, for when he felt around on the ground in front of him, he discovered a cluster of sharp, spiked metal objects. He picked one up and examined it. An ugly little thing, it consisted of five spikes sticking out from a small center. Whichever way it landed on the ground, two spikes would always point upward, ready to pierce the feet of anyone who stepped on it. They must have been strewn here by the man Seikei had been pursuing.

Gingerly Seikei took off his sandals and removed the spiky things that were caught in them. Fortunately he wasn't badly hurt—the thick straw sandals had been enough protection.

Still, as he limped back down the alley, Seikei felt ashamed that he had failed to carry out the task that the judge had given him.

To his surprise, however, the judge was not there waiting for him. Along with his own horse and Seikei's, he had disappeared. Seikei looked up and down the street, wondering what to do. The judge had left him on his own before, but usually he provided some kind of instructions before doing so.

"Follow the path." For some reason, those words popped into Seikei's head. Often, the judge used them to describe his method of capturing a criminal. Well, the path had led through the alley, but Seikei wasn't able to get through. What if he went *around?*

Seikei turned at the next corner and went up to the street on the other side. As he reached it, he looked down to the place where the alley came out. He saw something truly astonishing: Judge Ooka was there, sitting on the outstretched form of the man who had fled down the alley.

The judge spotted Seikei at the same time and gestured for him to hurry. Seikei ran. "Where have you been?" the judge asked when he approached. "I expected you to come out of the alley."

"There were sharp things in there that hurt my feet," Seikei explained.

"Tatsuno!" said the judge, giving a sharp slap across the shoulders to the man he was sitting on. "Did you scatter *tennen-bishi* in there?"

"I'm sorry," said Tatsuno in a voice that was slightly muffled because he was facedown on the ground. "Anyway, they were small ones."

"Why did you try to run away?"

"I didn't see who you were. I thought someone might be trying to rob me."

"Rob *you*?" The judge laughed, rocking back and forth and making Tatsuno all the more uncomfortable. "It's usually the other way around, isn't it?"

"That was a misunderstanding," Tatsuno said. "And anyway, I didn't harm anyone."

"You wouldn't have been inside Lord Inaba's castle the night before last, would you?" the judge asked.

"Oh, no, Your Honor," said Tatsuno. "I had nothing to do with that."

"With what?"

"Why, everyone has heard that Lord Inaba was killed," said Tatsuno. "It's the talk of Edo."

"Killed by a ninja?"

"That's how it is," Tatsuno said with a touch of self-pity. "If something bad happens, everybody wants to blame a ninja."

"Tatsuno is a ninja," Judge Ooka informed Seikei.

"He *is*?" Seikei took a second look at the thin man, now dusty and a little scraped here and there. He certainly wasn't what Seikei had imagined when his mother had frightened him with tales of fierce ninjas.

"I've retired," said Tatsuno with dignity. "I'm a teacher now."

"Fetch a rope," the judge told Seikei. "We must tie him so he won't try to escape."

Tatsuno protested loudly. "There is no need for that," he said in a silky voice. "None at all. How could anyone ever escape from your lordship anyway?"

"They couldn't, but I don't want to waste my time chasing you," said the judge.

"You won't have to do that, Your Honor."

"I have a task for you," the judge said.

Tatsuno hesitated. "What sort of task?"

"Get the rope," the judge told Seikei again, pointing to his horse, which had a coil of rope in back of the saddle.

"All right!" Tatsuno shouted. "I'll do it, whatever it is."

"And you won't try to escape again?" asked the judge.

"No."

"I have your word of honor as a ninja?"

"Yes, yes, my word of honor."

The judge stood up, and slowly, quite slowly, Tatsuno picked himself up from the ground. As he dusted himself off, Seikei saw that he wore a perpetually wary look, as if he were afraid something terrible were about to happen. Or perhaps that was just the effect the judge had on him.

"What's the task?" Tatsuno asked.

"First we're going to the prison," said the judge.

"I thought we had an agreement," said Tatsuno, dismayed.

"We do. We're not going to leave you there—unless I receive some information I don't expect. We're just going to visit some prisoners."

The judge mounted his horse. Seikei could never

understand how he did that so easily, as heavy as he was. After Seikei got on his own horse, Tatsuno said, "You know, that horse looks strong enough to carry both of us."

"You walk along next to me," the judge told him. "I want to know what else you've heard about Lord Inaba's murder."

The way Tatsuno told it, he had heard nothing about Lord Inaba's murder. He'd even forgotten who told him about it in the first place. "Probably someone in a sake shop," he said. "You know people will say anything there, true or not."

Finally, the judge said to him, "The evidence at the scene of the crime indicates that a ninja was the assassin."

"Didn't I tell you?" Tatsuno responded. "Whenever anything bad happens—"

"No one saw the killer," the judge interrupted, "not even the guards. And he escaped by lowering a rope from a high window."

Tatsuno shrugged. "Could be someone trying to throw blame on the ninjas. These days, people pick up a trick or two and think that's all there is to being a ninja."

"Where were *you* the night before last?" the judge asked.

"Me, Your Honor?" Tatsuno seemed deeply hurt by the question. "I was sound asleep at my cousin's house."

"Where is that?"

"In the Hongo district, far from Lord Inaba's castle."

"I'm sure your cousin will confirm what you've said."

"He'd better. Er . . . certainly he will, Your Honor."

The prison was a complex of ugly gray stone buildings that sent a thrill of fear through Seikei every time he saw them. They occupied as much land as a small farm and were as difficult to enter as any daimyo's castle. The three of them had to cross a moat, pass through a guarded gate in the massive outer wall that surrounded the entire prison, and then cross a second moat.

Even though the guards recognized Judge Ooka as one of the shogun's high officials, they kept him waiting until the warden emerged from somewhere in the main building. The warden was a member of the Ishide family, who had operated the prison ever since the first Tokugawa had become shogun. Only the Ishides were willing to do the job.

The judge told Ishide-san that he wanted to see the two men who had guarded Lord Inaba.

Ishide-san shook his head. "We have had to chain them for their own protection," he said. "They keep trying to kill themselves. If you sentence them to death, they will carry out the task."

"For now, I wish only to speak with them," said the judge.

The warden led them to one of the cleaner-looking

buildings. Here, Seikei knew, prisoners of samurai status were kept. Each had a cell to himself, and if they had money, they could order food and other luxuries from outside the walls.

Lord Inaba's two samurai had no luxuries. Kept in the same cell, each had his legs chained to the wall. A second chain bound their arms behind their backs. As soon as the judge saw them, he said, "Free their arms."

The warden started to object, but shrugged and said, "It is by your order."

The men hardly moved as he unlocked their chains. The judge stood in front of them and asked, "You were the two men assigned to guard Lord Inaba's bedchamber?"

"Yes, Your Honor," they said together. One of them added, "We should have committed seppuku as soon as we learned what happened." The other nodded and said, "Would your lordship have mercy and allow us that honorable death now?"

"Answer my questions first," the judge replied. "You don't appear to be careless men. Did you fall asleep that night?"

The two prisoners hung their heads. "We did," said the first man, "though it seemed more like an enchantment than sleep."

"Why do you say that?" asked the judge.

"Because I dreamed of a fox," recalled the man. "A fox that spoke to me. It didn't seem strange, not at all like a dream. That was why, when I awoke later, I thought a fox had gotten into Lord Inaba's room."

As the man spoke, Seikei noticed that his story was having an odd effect on Tatsuno. He nearly jumped at the mention of the talking fox, and now he looked at the judge as if he wanted to say something urgent.

"I know," the judge murmured, calming Tatsuno somewhat. "I remember."

The judge turned his attention to the prisoner again. "What did the fox say to you?"

The man thought for a moment and looked puzzled. "You know, I can't remember," he said. "It seemed like quite a pleasant conversation, as if we were somehow friends."

"I remember," said the second prisoner. The first one looked at him in surprise, and the second one said, "I was too ashamed to tell before now. I had the same dream. The fox kept telling me what a brave, vigilant samurai I was—truly a faithful retainer of Lord Inaba. . . ." He paused, swallowed hard, and added, "Lies. The fox lied to me."

"Perhaps not," said Judge Ooka. "I understand that there were many guests at Lord Inaba's castle that night."

"Yes. He had just returned to Edo for the year and many of his friends were invited."

"And his enemies?"

"Lord Inaba had no enemies," the prisoner said firmly. The other one nodded his agreement.

"Another question then," said the judge. "Did you have anything to eat or drink at the party?"

The two men were silent, and Seikei guessed the answer. "Only a little sake," the first prisoner said finally. "Just one cupful. It was not strong enough—"

The judge interrupted him. "Who served it to you?"

"Why . . . a wine steward. Come to think of it, he tried to serve me several times before I accepted."

"One of the regular household servants?"

"No, this was someone new. A fat man, very eager to please."

"Did he look like this man?" The judge pointed to Tatsuno, whose face grew more wary than before.

"No, I told you the steward was fat. This man is thin."

"This man knows how to change his appearance," said the judge. "Study his face."

The prisoner did so, carefully. "No, I'm sure it wasn't him. The steward was older than this man, although their faces were somewhat similar."

"You agree?" the judge asked the other prisoner, who nodded and added, "This man would never have been admitted to Lord Inaba's castle. He looks like a beggar."

Seikei saw a look of satisfaction on Tatsuno's face. He was no beggar, for certain, Seikei thought.

"I have one other thing for you to look at," the judge

told the two samurai. He reached into his kimono and drew forth the paper butterfly.

There was an audible gasp from Tatsuno. Everyone but the judge looked at him. He was almost choking with surprise—and, Seikei thought, with fear as well. The judge never turned his head, but a small smile crept across his face as he held the butterfly out for all to see.

5 —
LOOKING FOR PAPER

You know what that butterfly means," Tatsuno was saying. "And you didn't tell me about it when you made me promise to carry out a little task for you."

"I didn't say it was little," replied the judge. "But it requires a ninja."

They had left the jail after the two prisoners confirmed what the judge already knew—the butterfly had not belonged to Lord Inaba. The assassin must have brought it with him.

Before departing, the judge had told the warden, "Release these two men and return their swords to them." The warden made no objection. But outside, Seikei asked, "Will they kill themselves after they get their swords back?"

"If they believe their honor demands it," said the judge.

"They should not have drunk the sake," Seikei said. "In Daidoji Yuzan's book, he says the conduct of a warrior should be correct at all times."

"That is true," said the judge. "Many fine and noble

things are written in that book, and in other books as well. But a man should be judged not by books but by what is in his own heart."

Tatsuno interrupted. "I'm no samurai," he said. "I'm not going out to commit suicide for you." That was when he made the comment about the butterfly.

Seikei was too curious. He had to ask, "What *does* the butterfly mean, anyway?"

"It means," said Tatsuno, "that the person who left it is uncatchable. In fact it would be worth your life just to try to catch him. Leave him alone."

"But you're a ninja," said Seikei. "How can you admit defeat?"

"With ease, I assure you," Tatsuno said. "A ninja lives to fight another day, unlike a samurai."

"No matter," said the judge. "I do not want you to capture the man who left the butterfly, Tatsuno."

"Then what *is* the task you want me to perform?"

"I will let you know soon," said the judge. "We have one or two more places to visit first."

"If we're going to the shogun's palace," said Tatsuno, "I will have to change into a better kimono."

"No need for that," said the judge. "We're going to see a papermaker." He glanced at Seikei. "Someone you know well."

At first Seikei didn't understand. But when they entered the district of Edo where the papermakers had their shops, he remembered the last time he had been here. It was shortly after Judge Ooka had adopted him, and Seikei had come to thank the person who had indirectly made that possible.

He had first met her on the night he and his father—his old father, the tea merchant—had stopped at an inn on the Tokaido Road. Restless, Seikei had gone to the terrace of the inn that night to view the stars. There he met Michiko, who was out for the same reason. To amuse him, she told Seikei a ghost story. One so frightening that later that night he lay restless on his sleeping mat, unable to sleep. And so, he had seen the ghost that had come to steal a jewel from a rich daimyo. In the morning, Michiko and her father were accused of being the thieves, and Judge Ooka had arrived to investigate. Seikei told what he had seen, and the judge gave him his first assignment. When the mystery was solved (with Seikei's help), Michiko and her father were cleared and the judge granted Seikei's wish to be a samurai.

From the outside, the little shop looked just the same as it had when Seikei had last visited. A blue banner over the front porch of the shop read OGAWA FINE PAPERS AND SCREENS. The beautiful calligraphy on the sign told Seikei that Michiko herself must have made it.

He and the judge dismounted and tied their horses to a railing in front of the shop. A servant girl, sweeping the porch, looked at them wide-eyed and rushed inside to announce the arrival of an important-looking samurai. A few seconds later, Seikei saw a pair of eyes peep through the crack in the slightly open door. They were eyes that he recognized: Michiko's.

As soon as the judge stepped onto the porch, the door opened wide and Michiko's father stood there, bowing low. Right behind him was Michiko, who also bowed, after a quick smile in Seikei's direction.

The judge, Seikei, and Tatsuno all bowed in return. In hardly any time at all, the servant girl appeared with a tray of tea and *manju* rice cakes. They all sat down in front of a small alcove. Hanging on the wall in a place of honor was a scroll with a poem written on it. Seikei recognized the calligraphy, the beautiful handwriting that the poet had used. It was by Basho, Japan's greatest writer. Because the calligraphy of a poet is almost as important as his words, the scroll was especially precious.

Seikei noticed Tatsuno looking at the scroll too. But it was not a look of admiration, like Seikei's. Seikei had the odd feeling that Tatsuno was appraising the scroll, wondering how much he could sell it for if he could somehow slip away with it.

Seikei was so disturbed by this that he almost didn't notice when Michiko's father, Ogawa-san, spoke to him. Seikei realized by the way the older man was smiling at him that it had been a compliment. "Thank you," said Seikei, bowing his head.

"Don't you agree?" Ogawa-san asked his daughter.

With shining eyes, she looked at Seikei for a moment, and then said, "I knew he had the heart of a samurai when he spoke out to save us from a false accusation, Father."

"You must be very proud to have such a fine son," Ogawa-san said to Judge Ooka.

"He has much to learn," said the judge, "but I approve of the fact that he does not allow himself to be discouraged."

Everyone nodded and exclaimed their agreement with that, even Tatsuno, who had known Seikei for only two hours. They're just being polite, Seikei thought. But he knew the judge would never tell a lie, so Seikei allowed himself a moment of pride in his foster father's approval.

The polite conversation continued for a while. Seikei knew the Ogawas wanted to sell the judge some of their paper. But it would be bad manners for them to bring up the subject before he did.

Finally the judge said to Ogawa-san, "I was very pleased with the quality of the writing paper that you were kind enough to sell me the last time we were here."

"We have just made a batch that I believe is even better," said Ogawa-san. He looked at his daughter. "Michiko, bring some samples for Judge Ooka to examine."

She went to another room and returned with several

sheets of creamy-white paper. She handed them to her father, who in turn gave them to the judge. Seikei could tell how proud father and daughter were of the paper, but of course they could not say so.

Their pride was justified. The smooth surface of the paper and the even quality of its color were pleasing to the eye. Seikei thought how it would feel to dip a brush into jet-black ink and splash it boldly across the paper, creating a beautiful new poem or painting.

The judge made complimentary remarks about the paper and then said, "Could you provide me with fifty sheets?"

Michiko and her father looked at each other. Fifty sheets, Seikei knew, was a large order for them. "We do not have that many sheets in stock," Ogawa-san said. "But we can make some in a few days."

"No hurry," said the judge. "I am working on a case that will require me to travel. When we return, I will send Seikei for the paper."

"I assure you, it will be the same quality as this," said Ogawa-san.

"I have no doubt of that," replied the judge.

"You have not even asked me what it will cost."

"I'm sure it will be a fair price. We won't discuss it."

"We are deeply grateful for your generosity," Ogawa-san said, bowing his head.

"Are you traveling far?" asked Michiko.

This was a somewhat bold question for a girl to ask, and her father waved his hand as if to rebuke her.

"I'm sorry," Michiko said immediately. "I ask only because I want to be sure we have the paper ready when Seikei returns."

She gave Seikei a smile that he imagined no one else saw.

"Do not apologize," said the judge. "It is good for young people to ask questions. And to be truthful, Ogawa-san, I came here hoping you could answer a question for *me*."

Ogawa-san gave his daughter a look that said, *You see what trouble you have gotten us into?* But he said to the judge, "Anything you wish to ask."

The judge took the butterfly from his kimono. Tatsuno eyed it warily, as if he feared it would come to life and fly off. "I wonder," said the judge to Ogawa-san, "if you know who made this paper."

Ogawa-san delicately took the butterfly from the judge. He turned it over in his hands. "It is stained," he said.

The judge nodded without saying what had stained it. "You may unfold it if you wish," he told Ogawa-san.

"That would be a shame," said Ogawa-san, "for it is a beautiful example of origami. Whoever folded this paper into the shape of a butterfly was an artist."

Michiko leaned over his shoulder to get a look, and

he said to her, "You see the way the grain slants? That's *gampi* fiber. Must be Bakkoro's, don't you think?"

"Yes, Father," she agreed.

Ogawa-san handed the butterfly back to the judge. "This kind of paper-folding looks like it was done at a shrine for some ritual. And the person who often makes paper for those purposes is a man named Bakkoro. But he lives in Shinano Province, far to the north. So that may take you out of your way if you are going on a journey."

"On the contrary," said the judge. "You have just told me the first place we must go on our journey."

6 —
A GIFT

May I give Seikei something to take on the journey?" Michiko asked.

"They will want to travel light," her father answered.

"It isn't heavy," she replied. "Come, Seikei, it's on a high shelf. I can't reach it by myself."

Seikei stood, and then looked at the judge, who smiled and said, "When a young lady offers you a gift, you should accept with thanks."

Michiko rose and opened the door to the next room. She gestured for Seikei to follow. Sliding the door shut after them, she said, "You have grown taller since I saw you last. Before, we were almost the same height. Now I come up only to your shoulder."

For some reason, this pleased Seikei, who hadn't realized how much he had grown. It crossed his mind to say to her, "You have become more beautiful than before," but he knew she would laugh at him for being so foolish.

Michiko said, "I wish you had time to tell me all the cases you have helped the judge solve."

"Not many, really," Seikei said. He was glad he didn't have to tell Michiko about the time he took a job in a teahouse where geishas met their customers. Maybe she would think that was shameful.

"And now you're going on a journey with him, but he doesn't know until he comes here just where you're going. Does he do things like that often?"

Seikei smiled. "Yes," he said. "He just says we have to follow the path wherever it leads."

"Oh, well, he is very wise," she said, "so I suppose that is why he is difficult for me to understand. It's strange though. Just before you arrived I was reading Basho's travel journal. You know, the one he made on his last journey?"

"Yes," said Seikei, "I have heard about it, but never read it."

"When you return for the paper, I will lend you my copy," she said. "Anyway, something I read made me think of you, traveling all over with the judge, solving crimes." She picked a small book from a shelf. The front and back bindings were beautifully decorated with red and yellow maple leaves. Seikei remembered that Basho's last journey had been in the fall of the year.

"Would you like to hear what he wrote?" Michiko asked Seikei.

He nodded, willing to listen to her read the entire book, but she turned the pages until she came to one passage. "Here it is," she said. "He describes how he worries because he has grown old, and he may no longer be able to endure the hardships of travel. Then he says: '*I reasoned with myself that when I set out on this journey to remote parts of the country, I was fully aware that I was risking my life. So even if I should die on the road, that would only be the will of Heaven. These thoughts somewhat restored my spirits.*' "

The great poet's words sent a chill through Seikei. Despite the fact that there was a charcoal burner in the room on this wintry day, he shivered.

Michiko seemed not to notice. "Do you not think that nobly expresses the spirit of the poet?" she asked.

"It does," he replied. And it was true. Though the passage was frightening in one way, Basho's acceptance of death was exactly the way a samurai should feel.

"Oh!" Michiko exclaimed. "I nearly forgot about your gift. It occurred to me when I thought of Basho's travel journal that you might like this. When Basho set out on his journey, he took with him a small writing kit." She pointed to the top shelf of a case against the wall. "There's one up there, but you'll have to take it down yourself."

It was a stretch for Seikei too, but he managed to reach the jet-black lacquered box. It was small—too small for a writing kit, he thought. But Michiko opened it and showed him he was wrong. Inside was a tray that held two writing brushes with collapsible handles.

Folded, they took up no more space than Seikei's thumb. When Michiko removed the tray, Seikei saw a small ink stick, a stone tray, and even a tiny bottle of water to make the ink.

"And look," said Michiko. She slid off the end of the box to reveal several tubes of paper. "It's very thin paper," she said, partially unrolling one of the tubes to show him, "but it holds the ink well without running. If you have the inspiration for a poem on your journey, you can write it down immediately, just as Basho did."

Seikei hardly knew what to say. "This is such a generous gift," he told her. "I have done nothing to be worthy of it."

"On the contrary," she said, "you proved yourself to be as brave and honest as any samurai."

Seikei bowed his head. "I hope you will always be able to say that."

Michiko started to reply, then hesitated. Seikei looked up, surprised, for she seldom was shy around him.

"I hope you won't think me too bold," she said, "but I had a strange feeling about that man you arrived with. Is he a friend of Judge Ooka's?"

"No," said Seikei, "no, I'm certain he isn't a friend."

"I am glad to hear that," Michiko responded, "for if he were, then I would not speak ill of him. But I feel you should be on your guard if you travel with him."

"What makes you say that?" asked Seikei, thinking

54

she too had seen the way Tatsuno looked at Basho's poem on the wall.

"It's a feeling I have," she said. "He makes me uneasy. Perhaps you will think me foolish, but I am seldom wrong about such things." She looked at the door to the next room. "We should return to the others now," she said. "Promise me you will return soon."

Seikei thought of Basho's words. "If Heaven wills it," he said.

After they left the shop, the judge gave Seikei a leather bag full of coins. "I have to follow a separate path in this case," the judge explained. "You must go to this papermaker Bakkoro. He lives in the town of Minowa in Shinano Province. Show him the butterfly"— he handed it to Seikei—"and ask for the name of the person who bought the paper it was made from."

"Do you think he will remember?" asked Seikei.

"This is special paper," said the judge, "used by shrines for religious purposes. To a papermaker's eye, each batch of paper is different. I think it is likely he will remember."

He turned to Tatsuno and said, "I want you to go with Seikei."

Tatsuno looked uncomfortable. "He doesn't need my help for such a simple task," he said.

"I want you to keep Seikei safe and teach him to think like a ninja," said the judge. Seikei's ears perked up at this. Just as he was finally learning to be a samurai, now he was to try being a ninja.

But Tatsuno told the judge, "I cannot teach him to be a ninja. That takes years of training."

"I wouldn't want him to become a ninja," the judge said, "but it will be useful for him to know about them."

Tatsuno shifted his feet uneasily, looking back and forth from Seikei to the judge. Clearly he was sizing up Seikei and not liking what he saw.

The judge asked, "Do you think he makes a good samurai?"

Tatsuno shrugged. "He's your son, so of course he's a good samurai."

"He is my adopted son. He used to be the son of a tea merchant."

Tatsuno gave Seikei a sharper look than he had before. "Well, I guess it would be easy enough to take him to Shinano and see this papermaker."

"But after you visit the papermaker," said the judge, "I want you both to continue on to Etchu Province."

"Where Lord Inaba's domain is?" said Tatsuno with a raised eyebrow.

"Yes. Disguise yourselves in some way. Talk to as many people as you can. Listen to what they say—rumors, accusations, gossip. I want to know what is being said about Lord Inaba's murder."

"What exactly do you want us to find out?" asked Tatsuno.

"I wish to learn who Lord Inaba's enemies were."

Tatsuno thought about this for a moment. "We won't have to capture anyone for you, will we?" he asked.

"No, Tatsuno. You are not looking for the fox. I merely want to know who sent the fox to Lord Inaba."

"Where will you be?"

"In the city of Nara, visiting the governor of Yamato Province."

Tatsuno sighed. "I knew it sounded too good to be true."

"And, Tatsuno, one more thing," the judge said.

"Yes?"

"If any harm comes to Seikei, there will be no place in Japan where you can hide from me."

7 —
IN DISGUISE

F ive days later, Seikei and Tatsuno were on the road to Minowa. Seikei had cut his hair and shed the garments that marked him as the son of a samurai family. He still carried his wooden sword as protection, but had left the horse at a stable when they entered Shinano Province, three days' ride north of Edo.

"Our story will be that we are pilgrims," Tatsuno told Seikei at the beginning of the trip. "We're going to visit the sacred mountains in Etchu. There are so many pilgrims on the roads that we will pass without notice. And it gives us an excuse to stop anywhere to ask for food or a place to sleep."

He gave Seikei a sly look. "I know that as the son of a merchant you're used to much finer things, but—"

"It won't bother me," said Seikei. "I'm the son of a samurai now. I followed a troupe of kabuki actors along the Tokaido Road by myself." He immediately felt annoyed with himself. It was beneath the dignity of a samurai to brag.

"Don't display that bag of money your father gave

you," Tatsuno said. "There are robbers and outlaws on the roads here. Maybe you'd better let me carry it for safekeeping."

"I am not so foolish as that," said Seikei.

Tatsuno retorted with a proverb: "A man who thinks he is smarter than anyone else is foolish indeed."

"No danger there," said Seikei, "for I know I will never be as smart as Judge Ooka."

"He too must meet his equal someday," said Tatsuno, "and I assure you he will if he ever finds the person who left that butterfly in Lord Inaba's room."

Seikei hesitated. He had been wanting to ask something, but didn't want Tatsuno to think he was ignorant. Now seemed to be his best chance of finding out. "What does the butterfly mean? Why does it make you afraid?"

"Aha," said Tatsuno. "You don't even know, do you? The judge sends you, his own son, on a mission like this and fails to tell you what danger you're in. And yet people admire him!"

"Everyone admires him," Seikei said fiercely. "And you *fear* him." Once again, Seikei regretted his rash words as soon as they were out of his mouth.

"It is only good sense," Tatsuno responded, "to fear someone who could have me executed on a whim. That is why—" Tatsuno cut himself off, demonstrating that he had greater self-control than Seikei.

"Why what?" prodded Seikei.

"No matter," said Tatsuno, waving away the thought with his hand. "I can tell you, however, that the person who left the butterfly did so to drive off the evil kami he had released by killing Lord Inaba."

Seikei was so surprised, he stopped walking and stared at Tatsuno. "But . . . that means he was a Shinto priest."

Tatsuno shook his head. "He does not devote his life to Shinto, as the priests do, but yes, he knows how to perform the Shinto rituals."

"I never heard of a priest killing people," Seikei said.

"I told you, he's not a priest," Tatsuno said. "Haven't you been paying attention at all? He's a ninja—the ninja who calls himself Kitsune: the fox."

Stung by the rebuke, Seikei seethed. He was more confused than ever.

After walking without speaking for quite a while, Tatsuno finally broke the silence. "It isn't fair, you know," he said.

"What isn't?"

"That I'm responsible for your safety and I'm supposed to teach you about ninjas. I suppose all you've heard is that ninjas wear black and sneak about killing people."

Seikei didn't want to admit that was true.

"And, of course, that ninjas have magic powers that they can use to make themselves invisible or defeat enemies just by waving their hands."

For Seikei, Tatsuno's words were like an itch that had to be scratched. "Can they really do that?"

"Certainly," Tatsuno said, "but that's only part of being a ninja. Centuries ago, when the emperor lived at Nara and the Fujiwara family were shoguns—"

"Wait," said Seikei, "I want to know how you become invisible."

"Why would you want to know that?"

"Well . . . it sounds interesting. It must be very useful in certain situations."

"It is, yes." Tatsuno spoke as if he became invisible whenever he liked.

Then Seikei realized something: "How come you didn't become invisible when I chased you into the alley? Then the judge couldn't have caught you."

"Well, I did, don't you remember? You couldn't see me in the alley, could you?"

"No, but that was only because you hid behind some crates."

"I may have given that illusion, but in fact I was invisible. After I lost you, I was off my guard and that is when the judge saw me."

"I don't believe you," said Seikei.

Tatsuno shrugged. "That's of no concern to me."

Seikei was annoyed. "If you can really become invisible, let's see you do it right now."

"It's not some trick to be performed for the amusement of crowds in the street," Tatsuno replied haughtily. "It requires a close connection with the nature kami."

Seikei laughed. He couldn't help himself. "And *you* have that connection?"

"When the occasion requires it," said Tatsuno with a nod.

"Yes, well, I hope to see that occasion," Seikei said.

"If you do," replied Tatsuno, "it will mean we are in grave danger."

As they proceeded onward, Seikei thought there was little chance of that. The road that led to their destination was lightly traveled. Seikei and Tatsuno passed only an occasional farmer or laborer, who looked at them without curiosity or threats.

Approaching the Akaishi mountains, Seikei had thought them beautiful. Even though the peaks were bare of snow, the green pines and the bare-branched maples that covered their sides made a striking combination. But now that the road led upward through those very trees, he was often tired and out of breath. The weather grew colder the higher they traveled, and Seikei wished he had worn warmer clothing. But all the other clothes he owned showed that he was the son of a well-to-do samurai.

He was determined not to ask Tatsuno to stop for a rest. But the older man showed no signs of tiring, putting one foot in front of the other as steadily as if he had just started on the journey.

The first night they stopped at a small shrine where three Shinto priests lived. Families from the surrounding area contributed rice and vegetables to support the shrine. Though the priests gladly shared their meal with the two guests, Seikei could see there was barely enough. Later, when he and Tatsuno attended the evening prayer ceremony, Seikei left a silver coin for the kami that lived inside the shrine. He knew it would allow the priests to buy themselves a fish or two for their meals.

The next morning, Seikei awoke to find that a heavy snow had fallen during the night. The tree limbs hung low with their blankets of white, and the ground appeared as fresh as it must have when the earth was new. Even so, the sight dismayed Seikei as he realized it meant the journey would be harder today.

The priests, however, were delighted. They prepared a special meal for breakfast, opening a jar of *daikon* pickles that had been stored away for a festive occasion.

Tatsuno explained. "They haven't had much snow this winter," he told Seikei. "Without snowfall, the mountain streams won't flow when spring comes, and the farmers around here wouldn't get their planting season off to a good start. That would reflect badly on the priests. It would mean the shrine kami wasn't pleased."

After breakfast, Tatsuno spoke quietly with one of the priests, who left and returned with some otter skins.

"We can tie these around our feet so they won't get cold in the snow," Tatsuno said.

"I should leave the shrine an offering for these," said Seikei.

"No need. I saw you leave the coin last night," Tatsuno told him.

"That was only for the food," Seikei said. "The otter skins are valuable."

"Yes, but the priests think it was our presence here that pleased the kami enough to send the snow."

Seikei was puzzled. "Why would they—did *you* tell them that?"

Tatsuno smiled. "I mentioned that you had a close connection with the kami of nature."

"I cannot allow myself to benefit from such a lie," said Seikei.

"It wasn't you who lied," Tatsuno replied. "Anyway, how do you know it was a lie? You were the only person who made an offering at the shrine last night, and this morning the kami showed he was pleased."

"I never pretended to be close to the kami."

"Showing your humility," said Tatsuno. "Yet another of your virtues. Wrap those skins around your feet. With luck we'll reach Minowa by nightfall."

8 —
THE PAPERMAKER

Minowa turned out to be a small, neat village poised on the edge of a high bluff. The view, when Seikei paused to turn and look at it, was breathtaking. He wanted to stop and use his writing kit for the first time, but Tatsuno pulled him onward.

"If we hurry, the papermaker will still be in his shop," said Tatsuno. "I don't want to be stranded out here with no place to stay for the night."

It was easy to find Bakkoro. Though his shop had no sign, the sharp, pungent smell of *tororo* seeds wafted through the doorway. The pulp of the seeds was one of the ingredients of fine handmade paper. Seikei had smelled that same odor, not nearly so strongly, in the Ogawas' shop. Michiko and her father made their paper in a separate room. Here in this mountain village, Bakkoro had one large room as a workshop. No doubt few, if any, customers entered from the street. He made paper to order for regular customers and sent it to them.

Even so, Bakkoro didn't look up when Seikei and

Tatsuno entered. He was just lifting a large bamboo frame from a vat of liquid paper—a mix of pounded wood fiber, tororo seeds, and water. Shaking the frame so that the excess liquid returned to the vat, the papermaker now held high the delicately thin, shimmering liquid sheet that would dry into paper.

The slightest mistake on his part at this stage would ruin not only the sheet he was holding, but all the sheets he had made today, for he had to place the sticky, half-dry new sheet exactly on top of the others resting on his worktable, so that each edge lined up as neatly as the side of a box.

As the papermaker turned to face the light from the window, Seikei saw that Bakkoro was very old. His face was deeply lined, and only a few strands of white hair grew across the top of his skull. Yet the expression on his face was one of perfect calmness, as if he had performed this action too many times to worry that he might do it wrong.

Bakkoro opened the bamboo frame, and one edge of the sticky paper brushed against the stack of sheets below it. It seemed to touch as lightly as a downy feather from a newborn chick. As Bakkoro leaned forward, the rest of the sheet rolled off the frame as smoothly as a turning wheel. The far edge fell perfectly aligned with the top sheet on the stack. Seikei exhaled, and realized that all this time he had been holding his breath in anticipation.

Bakkoro set the now-empty frame down, and finally seemed to notice Seikei and Tatsuno. "How may I help you?" he asked.

"We are here by the authority of Judge Ooka, official investigator of the shogun Tokugawa Yoshimune," Tatsuno announced in a voice that was needlessly loud.

Seikei was startled. He didn't like Tatsuno assuming such high authority for himself.

Bakkoro's face still wore the same placid expression. "I am very honored to have you visit my humble workshop," he said. "Does the judge wish you to bring him some paper?"

"No," said Tatsuno. He snapped his fingers in Seikei's direction. "Show him the butterfly."

Seikei nearly refused. He resented Tatsuno's tone, which was one that he might use to a particularly slow-witted servant. But this was what they had come to find out, so Seikei fought back a retort and took the butterfly from his kimono.

Bakkoro turned his eyes upon it, then looked at Seikei as if asking permission to handle it. In response Seikei held it closer to the old man.

He picked it up and gave a chirp of disapproval when he saw the bloodstain on it. Delicately he took hold of each wing and pulled slightly to see the inside. Peering within the body of the butterfly, he nodded slightly.

"Is this your paper?" asked Tatsuno.

"I made it, if that is what you mean," Bakkoro responded.

"Who bought it from you?"

Though Tatsuno barked out his questions as if he were the judge and Bakkoro a prisoner, the old man's composure remained unshaken. He didn't hurry with his answer: "I don't ask my customers for their names."

"You must know their names if you send the paper to them—if you made it for a shrine, for example."

"I make paper like this for many shrines. The priests shape it into creatures that attract the kami." Bakkoro smiled. "Or make the kami go away, as this one was intended to do."

"You know the purpose of the butterfly?"

"Of course. It is used to purify a place where the kami of a dead person has been."

"You smile," Tatsuno said. "Do you find that amusing?"

"No. I expect that I myself will be dead before too long. It will be interesting to see where I go after that."

"We can make that happen sooner instead of later if you prefer," said Tatsuno in a voice filled with menace.

Seikei could no longer restrain himself. "That's enough!" he shouted.

He turned to Bakkoro. "We will not harm you," he said. "But we're trying to find a murderer. He left this butterfly near the man he killed. Won't you help us?"

Bakkoro looked at Seikei. His eyes were kind, but

there was sadness behind them too. A sadness that gave Seikei the uneasy feeling that it was meant for him. The old man handed the butterfly back to Seikei. "This paper," he said, "was made for the O-Miwa Shrine at the base of Miwayama."

Seikei took the butterfly, but then Bakkoro's hand moved—swifter than a leaping frog—and gripped Seikei's wrist. Seikei could feel the bones of Bakkoro's fingers, for the old papermaker's flesh was as thin as paper itself.

"But you must not go there," Bakkoro said.

Tatsuno was still angry as they left the town. "You shamed me by interrupting my line of questions," he told Seikei.

"You had no right to threaten him that way," said Seikei, who was in no mood to apologize. "You're not one of the shogun's officials."

"The papermaker didn't know that, did he?" Tatsuno shot back. "Anyway, we were sent here by one of the shogun's officials, so it's practically the same thing. I was just trying to find out what the judge wanted to know."

"He didn't want you to threaten people."

"How do you know? He wanted us to find out where that paper came from. The old man pretended he didn't know. Well, *I* know how to turn a fish into a songbird."

"He told us anyway," Seikei pointed out.

"Lucky for you," Tatsuno said. "And I hope you paid attention to the last thing he said too."

"About not going there? Where is the O-Miwa Shrine, anyway?"

"In Yamato Province. The shrine has no *honden,* no sanctuary for the kami to stay in."

"Why not?"

"Because the kami resides in the sacred mountain, Miwayama. There's a *torii,* a gate on the side of the mountain, but it's forbidden to go any farther than that."

"You sound as if you've been there."

Tatsuno didn't say anything for a while, unusual for him. Seikei was curious.

"*Have* you?" he asked.

"Yes," Tatsuno said quietly. "I first visited it with my teacher, many years ago."

"What is there about it that makes you afraid?"

"Nothing," replied Tatsuno, but Seikei did not believe him.

Seikei thought about what he had learned. Yamato Province. The judge had told them to meet him at the governor's house in Yamato Province. Did he know already that was where the butterfly had come from? If so, why did he order Tatsuno and Seikei to go on to Etchu Province to investigate the enemies of Lord Inaba?

Seikei sighed and marched on. The judge had sent him before on journeys whose purpose was unclear. It was not up to Seikei to ask why, but to obey. In the end, he was sure, the judge would reveal the reasons behind his instructions.

A gust of wind blew up, sending icy flakes of snow against their faces. In the howl of the gale, Seikei thought he heard the voice of the old papermaker, urging him to go back.

BLAZING SKIN

Seikei was not used to walking in otter skins, and somewhere on the road to Etchu Province, he slipped and fell. He twisted his ankle badly, and Tatsuno examined it. "Put it into the snow," he said. "That will keep it from swelling."

Seikei thrust his bare foot into a snowbank. The cold immediately numbed it, and the ankle seemed to stop throbbing. In a little while, though, Tatsuno told him to take his foot out of the snow. "But it feels better this way," Seikei protested.

"Maybe so, but if it freezes solid, it will break off and you won't have a foot to walk on," said Tatsuno.

Walking was easier for a while, but then Seikei's ankle began to hurt again, and he had to hobble. Finally, Tatsuno found a heavy branch on the ground. He broke it at a fork so that Seikei could use it as a crutch. They spent the night in a farmer's storage shed, and the next day, the ankle was worse than ever. Seikei gritted his teeth and forced himself to go on, even though the snow was now deeper than before. From time to time they would stop so Seikei could untie his otter-skin boot and dip his foot into the soothing snow.

While they were stopped this way, a tradesman passed by, leading a horse loaded with sacks of rice. When he saw what was wrong, he told them the next town was very close, only two hills beyond where they were. Better yet, the town had a doctor. "Look for the third house on the left from this end of the village," the man said. "His office has no sign, because everyone knows where he lives."

Seikei struggled to his feet, put the crutch under his arm, and gamely went on. The thought that some relief was close by encouraged him. As they reached the crest of the second hill, he saw the village below. It wasn't large—perhaps twenty houses in all.

The doctor here isn't likely to be a skilled man, Seikei thought. But at least I can go into a heated house and rest.

When they reached the doctor's house, they had to knock twice before anyone opened the door. Then the doctor himself stood there—a middle-aged man who looked sleepy. He gave Seikei and Tatsuno a long look, one that indicated strangers seldom came to his door. "I am Genko, a physician," he said finally. "Have you hurt your leg?" he asked Seikei. "Come inside and let's have a look at it."

They learned that he had in fact been sleeping when they arrived. "One of the villagers' wives had twins last night. Bad luck for her."

That *was* bad luck, Seikei thought. The judge had told him not to believe in superstitions, but everyone knew that twins were likely to bring trouble on a family.

"Anyway, she didn't die," the doctor said. "I don't know if that's good fortune for her—or bad. How'd you hurt yourself?" he asked Seikei.

"I fell and twisted my ankle."

"Best thing would be to rest until it gets better."

"We can't do that," said Tatsuno. "We have to get to Etchu Province."

"Here's good news for you then," said Dr. Genko. "You're *in* Etchu Province. What is your business here?"

Tatsuno was a little surprised. "We're . . . on our way to visit the shrine," he said. Seikei noticed the slight hesitation, and hoped the doctor wouldn't.

"Shrine?" Dr. Genko seemed puzzled. "We have many shrines, of course, but none that are famous."

"Well," said Tatsuno, motioning toward Seikei, "his father made a vow to go to the shrine in Kanazawa. But now he is ill and dying." He turned away from the dark look Seikei was giving him, and continued, "So we are fulfilling the pledge on his behalf."

"Ah, Kanazawa," said the doctor, nodding. "That's where Lord Inaba's castle is. You must mean the shrine there that honors Hachiman."

74

"Yes, that's it," said Tatsuno.

The doctor looked at Tatsuno. "Well, it's quite a distance from here," he said. He turned toward Seikei. "I don't think you'll make it on that ankle. Let's have a look at it." He motioned for Seikei to sit down on a long table.

As Seikei climbed up, the doctor took a wire frame from his pocket. Inside the frame were two shiny transparent disks. At first Seikei thought they were jewels, but a closer look showed that they were flat and thin. Seikei was further surprised when the doctor attached the frame to his face, adjusting it so that the jewel-like objects were in front of his eyes.

The effect was startling. The doctor's eyes appeared to be larger than before. "Is that magic?" Seikei asked.

Dr. Genko smiled and gently took hold of Seikei's foot. "Once," he explained, "when I was on a journey to Nagasaki, I was asked to treat a captain of one of the foreign ships that the shogun allows to trade there. The captain came from a distant place called Netherland, as I recall. A doctor had sailed with him, but died on the voyage."

He sniffed. "Some doctor. As it happened, I was able to cure the captain. He wanted to reward me, but I had no use for his money, of course. So I saw him using this device on his face, and asked what its purpose was. It makes objects appear much larger, and so I thought it would be useful to me in my work. He generously gave it to me. Apparently such devices are common in his country. Now, hold still. Let me know when you feel pain."

Seikei gritted his teeth as the doctor turned his foot, first to one side, then the other. He was determined to withstand the pain without complaining.

"Doesn't that hurt?" Dr. Genko asked.

Seikei shook his head no, not trusting himself to speak without showing the pain.

"It's very swollen," said Dr. Genko. "Have you taken any herbs to dull the pain?"

Seikei shook his head again.

"How about if I do this?" asked the doctor with a sudden movement.

Seikei let out a yell. He couldn't help himself.

"Ah. I thought *that* would hurt," said Dr. Genko. "Stay there for now. I'll fix something to make it feel better."

It had felt better *before* the doctor took hold of it, Seikei thought. He looked around, wondering if he could persuade Tatsuno to leave now. But Tatsuno was looking at a beautiful lacquered box that rested on a shelf against the wall. It occurred to Seikei that Tatsuno might slip it into his sleeve when no one was looking.

But Dr. Genko noticed him too. "That box holds my dragon bones," he said. "Some people think you'll die within a year if you touch them."

Tatsuno took a step backward. "Why do you keep them here, then?" he asked.

"Others believe that they make an excellent medicine. I use them when all else has failed."

"And do they work?" Tatsuno said, eyeing the box again.

"As well as my other cures," said Dr. Genko. "Some people live and some die." He looked at Seikei. "I think you will live."

Dr. Genko took a porcelain flask from another shelf, removed the lid, and sprinkled some silvery powder into his hand. Folding back Seikei's kimono, the doctor placed a pinch of the powder at three different places along his leg.

"You don't mind a little pain, eh?" the doctor said to Seikei. His eyes, behind the clear jewels, made him look like an owl about to pounce on a mouse.

"No, I don't mind," Seikei said in a voice that wasn't as steady as before.

The doctor took three burning incense sticks from a bowl of sand. He handed one to Seikei and kept the other two. "When I give you the signal," he said, "touch the burning end of the stick to the powder above your knee, there." He pointed.

Seikei tensed, wondering what would happen. The doctor held the other two sticks above the small piles of powder lower down on Seikei's leg. "Now," he said.

As soon as the burning sticks touched the powder, showers of sparks and flame shot into the air. Seikei gasped, because all this was happening on *his* leg.

Then the sparks died down, leaving only three small clouds of pleasant-smelling smoke. Seikei was even more surprised. "That didn't hurt!" he said.

The doctor nodded. "Many people imagine it will, and because of their fear, it does."

Seikei noticed the echo of what Judge Ooka had said about fear of torture. He almost told the doctor about it, but remembered that he and Tatsuno were supposed to be disguised as pilgrims.

"And how does your ankle feel now?" the doctor asked him.

Seikei wiggled his foot. "The pain is gone," he said, astonished.

"Yes, but it will return," said the doctor. "The powder stops pain for a while, but does not cure. Only rest will heal your ankle." He took a white linen cloth from a chest and tied it tightly around Seikei's ankle. "Use that when you must walk," he said, "but stay off your feet as much as possible."

"We have to go to Kanazawa," Tatsuno objected.

"You should not be in such a hurry," the doctor said. "Kanazawa is a bit unsettled now, because Lord Inaba has died. His son Yutaro has arrived to claim the allegiance of his father's samurai."

"He's here already?" said Seikei.

"So I am told," the doctor said. "I have not yet seen him. If he chooses to inspect his domain, he would not come to such an insignificant, out-of-the-way village as this."

He paused, then added, "There is a family here that will welcome you. The husband and wife are very devout, and they would believe they are gaining merit by sheltering two religious pilgrims such as yourselves."

"I guess we can spare a day or two," said Tatsuno.

"I will take you to their house," said Dr. Genko. "Just one thing," he added.

"What?"

"I would not mention to them that you are going to the shrine of Hachiman at Kanazawa."

"Why not?"

"There is no shrine of Hachiman at Kanazawa."

10 —
PRAYERS FOR MOMO

In a gray and sunless twilight, Dr. Genko walked down the street with Seikei and Tatsuno. Even the dimming light could not hide the fact that the house they stopped at was badly in need of repair. Bare patches could be seen in its high thatched roof. The paper in a front window had been torn and pasted together instead of replaced. A board on the front steps was broken, and the doctor told them to be careful because another, on the porch itself, was loose.

If it hadn't been for the candlelight that shone dimly through the window, Seikei might have thought the house deserted. But after a long wait, a man answered Dr. Genko's knock. He looked in need of repair himself. His cheek bore an ugly sore that looked as if it hadn't healed in a long time. His hands seemed twisted from years of hard work.

"Joji," Dr. Genko said, "these are travelers on their way to Kanazawa. They need a place to stay while the boy's ankle heals."

The man slid the door open wider. "You are welcome here," he said.

Inside, Seikei was surprised to find that there were no *tatami* mats covering the floor. Most of the house consisted of a single large room. In the center was a pit in which a small fire burned, giving barely enough heat to be felt at the doorway.

Sitting on a rice-paper mat by the fireplace was a woman who stared into the flickering flames as if trying to read a message in them. As soon as Seikei entered the room, he felt her eyes turn toward him, shining out of the darkness. They followed him carefully as he approached the fire. Then, apparently disappointed in what she saw, the woman again lowered her eyes to the smoky pit.

Her husband said, "I am Joji, and this is Sada." Seikei and Tatsuno introduced themselves, using only their first names, as people in the countryside did.

Seikei realized that most of the light in the room did not come from the fireplace. Around the walls were many small shrines with statues of Buddhas and Buddhist saints. In front of each, a candle was burning.

Two small pots hung from hooks on a metal bar over the fireplace. "We were about to eat," Joji explained. "You are welcome to share all that we have."

Seikei was ashamed to take their food when he saw how little there was. One pot contained some roots and rice boiled in so much water that it had turned to mush; the other held boiling water for tea. Seikei claimed not to be hungry, but Joji gave him a little of the rice mixture in a bowl anyway. Seikei gratefully accepted a cup of the tea, but when he tasted it, his mouth puckered. He realized it had been made from ground acorns with a few tea leaves added.

Joji made a few polite attempts at conversation during the meal, but Sada remained silent. From time to time, her eyes lifted and flashed at Seikei for a second, making him uncomfortable.

Tatsuno must have felt the same way, for when he finished eating, he volunteered to go outside and bring in more firewood. "We have none," Joji told him. "When it is daylight, I will go look for some."

"But you can't let the fire go out," Tatsuno said. "It will be a lot of work to start it again tomorrow."

"We cover the coals with ashes," Joji said. "Usually they burn so slowly that the fire lasts through the night. Come join us in prayer now. That's more important."

Seikei could see Tatsuno didn't agree, but since they were posing as religious pilgrims, he could hardly refuse.

The four of them knelt before each of the room's Buddhist shrines in turn, while Joji led them in prayer. Seikei had attended Buddhist temples with his father the merchant, who believed that it did no harm to appeal to all religions. So Seikei knew enough to chant, "All praise to the Amida Buddha," along with Joji and Sada. Even Tatsuno knew that much. Amida was a person who, long ago, achieved enlightenment and now resided in the Pure Land. But before he left, he had promised to return to help anyone who called his name.

As Seikei listened to Joji and Sada express their wishes, he realized they were not asking Amida's help for themselves—even though it looked like they could use it. Instead they were praying for someone named Momo. Sada's cheeks were covered with tears when they finished. She turned away from the two guests and lay down on a mat against the wall.

Joji prepared for sleep as well. After tamping down the fire, he told Seikei and Tatsuno they could sleep close to the hearth, where the stone would stay warm throughout the night. Seikei noticed that the man made sure to lock the door to the porch—a silly precaution, Seikei thought, because both the door and windows were so flimsy that an intruder could easily break in. Anyway, what was there to steal?

Joji opened a privacy screen in front of the section of the floor where he and his wife would sleep, and then retired. In a short time, Seikei could hear Tatsuno snoring on the other side of the hearth. The lighted candles flickered in their puddles of molten wax, casting odd shadows around the room.

For a while Seikei himself slept. When he awoke, some of the candles had guttered out. He realized that his ankle hurt again; the pain had awakened him. It was not yet morning. The others' heavy breathing told him they were still asleep. He shifted his foot, hoping to ease the pain. But it only got worse, throbbing now as if it were the only thing alive in the room.

He wished he could go to Dr. Genko for another treatment. No, Seikei told himself, there was no sense bothering him for what was only pain. Pain was something that a samurai should ignore.

He shifted again. Even though the room was cold, he felt warm and feverish. Maybe he was too close to the hearth. Sighing, he sat up. Now he was too restless to sleep.

An idea came to him. Before, placing his ankle in snow had numbed it. He would try it again. Getting to his feet, he hobbled to the door. At first it refused to open, and then Seikei remembered that Joji had locked it. Finding the latch in the darkness took him a little while, but he finally undid it.

The door slid uneasily on its track. Seikei prayed that the entire door frame wouldn't fall with a crash onto the wooden porch. As soon as it opened a little, he slipped outside.

His otter-skin boots were still on the porch, but he didn't need them. Several inches of snow lay on the ground right up to the edge of the porch. He sat down there and lowered his foot, cracking through the icy crust that had formed on top of the snow during the night.

He felt relief at once and leaned back. The night was bright and clear. All around him, the snow-covered trees glowed. High above, a full moon shed its light upon the scene.

All at once, Seikei knew that he must write a *haiku* to describe what he saw. Fortunately the writing kit Michiko had given him was small enough for him to take everywhere. He reached into his kimono and brought it out.

Rubbing the ink stick onto the stone tray, Seikei had the idea of using snow to make the ink. He scraped up a little and swirled it into the tray with one of the brushes. It almost made him giddy—this was just the sort of thing Basho would do!

But now, the hard part. He was not the poet Basho was, but he had to write something worthy of the scene. If he could not, it was better to destroy the paper and forget he had ever tried.

Words came into his head as he unrolled a sheet of paper. Swiftly and with as little hesitation as possible, he pressed the ink-laden brush onto the empty sheet.

I step into the moon
The snow falls to earth
Yet I soar through the sky

"We keep the door locked at night." The voice was right behind Seikei, and came so unexpectedly that he jumped. As he did, he put all his weight on his sore ankle and cried out.

"Are you all right?" It was Sada. She had come up behind Seikei while he was concentrating on the poem.

The poem! He had dropped the paper, and now saw it in the snow. Facedown.

As he picked it up, the paper shredded, leaving him with a jagged, running mess. Perhaps it was a sign, he thought. That the poem was not good enough.

"We keep the door locked at night," the woman said again. This annoyed Seikei more than it should have. "Why?" he asked in a not-too-polite tone. "Who around here would want to steal from you? And what would they steal?"

She said nothing for a moment. Her head turned slightly so that the moon caught her eyes, and Seikei saw once again, uncomfortably, that she was looking at him. "Momo," she said. "They stole Momo from us."

11 —
LORD INABA'S
ENEMIES

Three days later, Dr. Genko inspected Seikei's ankle and pronounced it well enough to walk on. That was good news to Tatsuno, who was bored and eager to move on.

Seikei would have stayed longer. His presence had seemed to breathe life into Sada. The old woman had treated Seikei kindly, unwrapping the bandage to massage his ankle and even bringing handfuls of snow inside to soothe it.

Seikei was curious about what had happened to Momo, who was Sada and Joji's daughter. But Sada had said no more about her, and turned away Seikei's questions. What happened to the girl remained a mystery.

Seikei and Tatsuno prepared to leave, thanking the old couple for their hospitality. Seikei left some coins where he knew they would be found after he left. Tatsuno noticed and shook his head disapprovingly. "If you pay them, they won't earn merit from performing an act of charity—that is, sheltering us."

Seikei saw the truth of this. He knew that Joji and

Sada would refuse the money if he tried to give it to them openly. An idea came to him. He would give the money to Dr. Genko instead. He in turn could use it to help villagers who were in need.

Dr. Genko accepted the money gladly. "This will mean more than you realize," he said. "Are you sure you can afford it?"

"Yes, take it," Seikei replied.

"If you don't mind," said Dr. Genko, "I will walk part of the way to Kanazawa with you. There is a farmer in that direction who has a cyst that needs draining from time to time."

The day was clear, and even though it was cold, Seikei was glad to breathe fresh air after three days in the smoky little thatched hut. After they were on the road for a while, Seikei asked Dr. Genko, "What happened to Joji and Sada's daughter?"

Dr. Genko looked at him. "What do you know about that?"

"She told me that her daughter had been stolen. That was all. They pray for her."

Instead of answering, the doctor asked, "Where are you from? Who are you? I know you're not pilgrims."

Tatsuno started to answer, but Seikei cut him off. He felt that the doctor's kindness deserved honesty.

"I am the son of Judge Ooka. He sent us here to find out who Lord Inaba's enemies were."

The doctor nodded and thought some more before

he spoke: "Some of Lord Inaba's men came through our village a year ago and saw Momo. She was a beautiful girl, too beautiful for a place like this. But she was innocent of the ways of men. The samurai carried her off and treated her shamefully. Later, we heard that she killed herself rather than return home in disgrace. That is why her parents pray for her."

Seikei was too shocked to say anything. He could not imagine samurai doing such an evil act.

"Would you say Joji and Sada are Lord Inaba's enemies?" Dr. Genko asked quietly.

"But they—*they* wouldn't have been responsible for killing Lord Inaba," said Seikei.

"Probably not," agreed Dr. Genko.

"And perhaps Lord Inaba never knew that his samurai acted this way."

"Look around you," said the doctor. "What do you see?"

Seikei let his eyes roam. The land was steep and hilly, sloping upward toward high peaks in the distance. Snow covered most of the ground, but here and there patches of it had been scraped away. Within the bare patches, Seikei saw what at first appeared to be small bundles of straw. All of them, however, were moving of their own accord. He realized that they were farmers wearing coats made of straw to protect them against the cold. Looking closer, Seikei saw that they were using hoes and spades and even sticks on the bare ground.

"Those people are digging," he said. "But why? It's not the right time of year to plant anything."

"They are looking under the snow for things to eat," said Dr. Genko. "Nuts, acorns, pinecones, roots—anything that will ease their hunger. They are starving."

"How could that be?" asked Seikei. "Aren't most of them farmers?"

"The rice crops have been attacked by insects two years in a row," said the doctor. "Almost nothing could be harvested."

"Even so," argued Seikei, "the lord of this domain should distribute food that has been saved from plentiful years."

Dr. Genko shook his head. "On the contrary," he said, "Lord Inaba's overseers demanded that the farmers pay their full taxes—one-fifth of the usual rice crop."

"But how could they pay if no rice had been harvested?" asked Seikei.

"By taking it from the rice that had been stored in previous years," the doctor replied.

"That cannot be true," said Seikei angrily. "How would they expect the farmers to live?"

"As you see," said the doctor, gesturing toward the people wandering through the snow-covered fields, "they expect the farmers to solve that problem by themselves."

Seikei was silent for a moment. He had not dreamed

that such injustices could exist in the shogun's realm. Perhaps there was a misunderstanding. What would the judge do?

"Have the peasants petitioned Lord Inaba?" Seikei asked. "Lord Inaba the father, I mean. I had heard that he was a kind man."

"So did the person who took the farmers' petition to Lord Inaba's castle," said the doctor. "That was why he volunteered to do so." The doctor paused. "He returned with his ears, nose, and lips cut off."

"This isn't *right!*" Seikei said. "The shogun wouldn't allow it. Someone should go to the provincial governor."

Tatsuno, who had been listening quietly, now snickered. "Excuse him," he said to the doctor. "He is only a boy."

Seikei felt stung. "But my father is one of the shogun's officials," he said. "I myself have met the shogun. I know that neither of them would approve of this."

Dr. Genko smiled sadly at Seikei and said, "Your friend knows that the chief aim of the shogun is to keep order in the country. He relies on daimyos like Lord Inaba to maintain a force of samurai who will preserve order. How they do that is up to them."

"But if people are starving, the proper order of things is upset," said Seikei. "A ruler has a duty to protect his people."

"I see you have read the ancient books," said the doctor. "But Edo is far away, and order here is preserved by force."

"When I see my father again, I will report to him what you have told me," Seikei said.

"Judge Ooka has a reputation as a just man," said the doctor. "So he sent you here to find Lord Inaba's enemies?"

"That's right."

"Look around you," the doctor said. "They are everywhere, digging in the snow to survive."

They left the main road at a narrow lane that led to a farmhouse, Seikei and Tatsuno following the doctor. Once, Seikei saw Tatsuno turn his head to look behind them. Seikei did the same and saw that others were following. He thought he recognized some of the people who had been scraping beneath the snow for food. But since they were all wearing straw coats, it was almost impossible to distinguish one from another.

Tatsuno gave him a glance and pointed to Seikei's wooden sword. Seikei knew what he meant, but he wasn't worried. He was sure Dr. Genko wouldn't lead them into a trap.

They walked around the farmhouse toward a larger building in back of it. As they passed the house, the front door slid open and two small children peeped out with large, solemn eyes. Someone pulled them back and shut the door quickly.

When they reached the larger building, Seikei saw that it was a storehouse for rice. Inside, however, he was surprised to find at least twenty men standing and stamping their feet to keep warm. Their clothing, rough cotton trousers and woven straw cloaks, showed that they were farmers. They carried hoes, pikes, axes, or spades—but Seikei had the definite impression that today they were not intended to be used as tools.

"We didn't invite strangers here," someone said loudly.

"I have faith in them," Dr. Genko said. "They may be able to carry our petition."

"To the new Lord Inaba?" another voice asked sarcastically. Bitter laughter echoed around the room.

"Perhaps," said the doctor. "Or to someone above Lord Inaba. They have come here on the orders of a person in the shogun's government."

That announcement only filled the room with sullen muttering. Seikei could make out a few words here and there: "Spies." "Who sent them?" "They're lying!"

One of the men stepped forward. He had powerful shoulders and looked as if he could uproot a tree all by himself. "What are you here for?" he asked.

Before Seikei could answer, Tatsuno said, "Show some respect! If you want our help, tell us what your grievances are. Supposing we believe you, we'll report them to the shogun."

The room fell silent. Seikei could tell the men wanted to trust him. "I had five children," the man in front of them said, "besides my wife and mother. We lost our whole rice crop this year because of the locusts. Then Lord Inaba's men came and demanded the taxes they said we owed. How can a man pay taxes if he has nothing to feed his own family?"

Tatsuno nudged Seikei. "Write that down," he commanded. Seikei looked at him in surprise, and Tatsuno gave a curt little nod.

Reluctantly Seikei took the writing kit from his kimono and prepared the ink. The farmers seemed reassured by the sight of it. Very likely, Seikei knew, none of them except Dr. Genko could read or write. To them the writing kit meant that Seikei and Tatsuno must, indeed, be important people.

One by one they all came forward to tell their stories. Each tale was much the same as the others, different only in details. But of course, Seikei reflected, each story was personal. One man gave the names of his children, and after that, they all did, as if writing down their names would help feed them. Another listed the names of family members who had died of starvation or illness. One man even mentioned the name of the horse that he had had to slaughter for food. He shed tears over the horse.

At first Seikei regretted using his precious supply of paper to write all this down. But as he heard the stories, he realized how important they were. He made up his mind that someone would listen to them. Seikei would make sure of it.

12 ~
A Fight

The farmers accompanied Seikei and Tatsuno back to the main road. Their mood was happier now, as if by giving their cares and complaints to Seikei to write down, they had—at least for the moment—gotten rid of them.

Dr. Genko sensed it. "You have given them hope," he said as he bade farewell to Seikei and Tatsuno.

"I will make sure their hopes are fulfilled," Seikei said earnestly.

Tatsuno and the doctor exchanged a glance. "Only a boy," Tatsuno reminded the doctor. Seikei pressed his lips together to keep himself from replying. He would show them.

The road continued northward, toward Lord Inaba's castle town, Kanazawa. By midafternoon they came to a fork, where another road led to the west. "We go that way," said Tatsuno.

"No, no," Seikei protested. "Kanazawa is up the other road, to the north."

"It certainly is," said Tatsuno, "and we have no reason to go there."

"But we must! We have to present the farmers' grievances to Lord Inaba."

"What do you think Lord Inaba will do then?"

"Why . . . I don't know. He should take steps to reduce their suffering."

"I can't believe you're this big a fool," said Tatsuno. He was not angry, merely stating a fact. "Your original father, the merchant, must have been happy to get rid of you."

Seikei's face reddened. Actually that was true. "But now," he said, "I am a samurai, and I would betray my honor if I didn't keep my word."

"To those farmers? You'd be doing them a favor if you threw those papers away. Better, burn them so no one will ever find them. Have you ever heard the expression 'The nail that sticks up gets hammered down'? If Lord Inaba knows their names, he'll come here and make their lives a lot more miserable than they are now."

"But if that's true," said Seikei, "then why did you have me write down all the complaints?"

"Because I wanted us to get out of there safely," Tatsuno said patiently. "Didn't you see all the tools they were carrying? The bamboo spears they had? Those farmers were in a mood to use them on someone, and we were the obvious choices."

"We aren't working for Lord Inaba."

"You don't know these country people, I see. We were strangers. That was all they needed to know."

"Nevertheless," said Seikei, "they trusted me and I accepted that trust. So I am going to Kanazawa, no matter what you choose to do."

He strode resolutely down the right-hand fork in the road. He didn't care whether Tatsuno followed or not. So far, there hadn't been any danger to speak of, and Seikei had once traveled halfway down the Tokaido Road by himself. Well, nearly by himself, Seikei had to admit. Bunzo had followed him, disguised as a holy man.

There wasn't any chance of Bunzo knowing where he was now.

Seikei cast a glance over his shoulder, just out of curiosity. Looking annoyed, Tatsuno was following him, about thirty paces back. Secretly Seikei felt a little relieved.

Some time later, they saw a horseman coming toward them. He was moving briskly, so they knew he must be a samurai. The farmers used their horses only for pulling carts or carrying loads.

As the rider drew closer, Seikei recognized the crest on his kimono. It was a camellia, the symbol of the Inaba family. Tatsuno nudged Seikei, who remembered that those of the lower classes were supposed to move to the side of the road when a mounted samurai passed by. For good measure, Tatsuno knelt, and Seikei did the same.

But the horseman did not pass them. Instead, he reined in his horse and turned to face them. "Who are you and where are you going?" he asked in a gruff voice.

"We are only pilgrims on our way to Kanazawa," said Tatsuno, sounding more like a beggar than a man on a holy mission.

"And we have a message for Lord Inaba," Seikei piped up. He felt Tatsuno cringe.

"A message, eh?" said the samurai. "What's it about?"

Before Seikei could answer, Tatsuno said in an even more sniveling voice, "Only our humble prayers for his late father, sir."

"Is that right? Give me the message. I'll deliver it to Lord Inaba myself."

Seikei heard Tatsuno curse under his breath. So did the samurai. "What's that?" he asked.

"Just a prayer for you too, sir," said Tatsuno.

"I want to see this message," the samurai said again. "Produce it at once."

Seikei reached into his kimono, but Tatsuno turned and grabbed his arm. "It's sacred," he explained desperately. "It must not be taken out in the open air."

The samurai's hand went slowly to the hilt of his long

sword. "I think you two are farmers trying to stir up trouble," he said. "That's what I was sent here to find out. Now show me this message or—"

With a piteous cry, Tatsuno threw himself on the ground in front of the horse. "Oh, sir!" he cried. "Exalted sir! Forgive us for carrying a message that might offend."

With each word, Tatsuno hobbled forward on his knees, drawing closer to the horse and rider. The horse, frightened by his cries, took a tentative step backward, but the samurai urged him forward until he was virtually on top of Tatsuno.

Then, quick as a snake's head striking, Tatsuno reached up and caught hold of the bridle around the horse's head. He pulled downward with all his might. The horse whinnied in fright and pain.

With a roar of anger, the samurai drew his sword. Once that happened, he was honor bound to use it, and Seikei reached for his own sword. Though it was only made of wood, he might help in some way.

Before he could do anything, however, the samurai took a mighty swing at Tatsuno's head—which suddenly disappeared. Seikei thought it must have been cut off, but then realized he had only ducked underneath the horse.

The samurai drew his short sword now, so that he had one in each hand. But he was having trouble keeping his balance. Tatsuno still had a grip on the horse's bridle and now was pulling the animal's head down and to one side. Though the horse struggled mightily to get away, Tatsuno was strong enough to hold him.

As Tatsuno emerged from beneath the horse, he dodged the animal's kicking legs. Then, surprisingly, Tatsuno stepped to one side and kicked the horse's left front leg.

The road was snowy and even though the horse wore straw shoes, the ground was slippery. When Tatsuno struck its leg, the horse lost its footing, and all three of them—the horse, the samurai, and Tatsuno—tumbled sideways to the ground with a great thud.

Still quick as lightning, Tatsuno was first to regain his footing. That was fortunate, for the samurai had kept his grip on his swords even though one of his legs was pinned underneath the horse. He swung out, first with one blade and then the other. Nimbly as an acrobat, Tatsuno ducked under the first blow, then jumped high in the air to escape the second. Nevertheless, the samurai's short sword sliced through Tatsuno's kimono, missing his legs only because Tatsuno spread them apart while still in the air.

When Tatsuno came down, he managed to land with one foot on the samurai's left arm, immobilizing it. The samurai gave one last desperate lunge with his other sword before Tatsuno stamped on that arm too. Wobbling on the writhing samurai, he called to Seikei: "Give me your sword."

Seikei tossed it to him without thinking, for a samurai should never give up his sword. Tatsuno used it nobly, however: Catching it on the fly, he brought the flat of it down hard on the samurai's head.

Tatsuno stepped off the samurai's arms and moved aside so the horse could get up. Seikei rushed to look at the samurai's still form. "Did you kill him?" he asked. That would be a shame, for Seikei himself had never used the sword to kill anyone.

"No," said Tatsuno, "but I'll soon take care of that." He pulled the long steel sword from the samurai's hand and raised it high, preparing to strike off the man's head.

"Wait!" shouted Seikei. "You can't do that! He's defenseless."

"Of course," replied Tatsuno. "That's why this is the time to do it. I would have killed him earlier, but as you may have noticed, *he* was trying to kill *me*."

"But what good will it do to kill him?" Seikei asked. "He's one of Lord Inaba's samurai. We don't want to offend the daimyo. We've got to take him this message."

"I recall suggesting some time ago that we stay as far away from Lord Inaba as possible," Tatsuno responded. "*You're* the one who wants to visit him."

"The judge would want us to go on to Kanazawa," said Seikei, "to see if we can find who might have been enemies of the old Lord Inaba."

"I should think we've already found enough of them," grumbled Tatsuno.

"I have an idea," said Seikei. "We'll take the samurai's horse. That way we'll get to Kanazawa faster."

"I'll take his kosode too," said Tatsuno. "Only fair, since he ruined mine."

Tatsuno liked the way the kosode fit so well that he also appropriated the samurai's two swords, tucking them under his obi. Seikei disapproved, but he had to admit Tatsuno had won them fairly in combat.

In fact, Seikei could hardly believe the way Tatsuno had overpowered the samurai. "I didn't know you could fight like that," he said.

"Never underestimate an opponent until you've tested him," said Tatsuno, tying his hair up in samurai fashion. "He might know *ju-jutsu*."

"What's that?" asked Seikei.

"A style of fighting developed by ninjas," Tatsuno said.

The horse shied away from Tatsuno, naturally enough, but it allowed Seikei to take it in hand. After Seikei had ridden it for a while, Tatsuno easily slipped on behind him.

"At this rate, we should have no trouble reaching Kanazawa by nightfall," said Seikei.

"That's what worries me," said Tatsuno.

13 ~
INTO THE CASTLE

As they approached the city walls, Seikei dismounted and walked alongside the horse, posing as Tatsuno's servant. Tatsuno found this more amusing than Seikei thought he should. With Tatsuno dressed in the samurai's kosode, they blended right in with the crowds in Kanazawa's streets. Every third person seemed to be wearing the colors of the Inaba family.

Seikei wanted to go to the castle right away. Tatsuno scoffed at him. "You think we'll just drop in and get to see Lord Inaba?" asked Tatsuno.

"I've *already* met him," Seikei pointed out. "He saw me with the judge and knows I work for him."

"Still, it's better to look things over before we rush into trouble," said Tatsuno. "Let's have a good meal for a change."

"We're supposed to be gathering information for the judge."

"Inns are the best place to learn things—if you have sharp ears," said Tatsuno.

Seikei could not deny that he'd learned a great deal about another case while serving as an attendant in a teahouse. So they stopped at a lively-looking inn. Tatsuno handed the horse's reins to a stable boy standing outside. Three samurai were having an argument on the porch. Tatsuno and Seikei tried to step by them, but one of them hailed Tatsuno. "Don't I know you?" he asked. The man's speech was slurred, and Seikei could tell he was somewhat drunk.

"I don't think so," Tatsuno answered.

"No, wait," the other man said. "Didn't you go with the new lord to Yamato Province last month?"

"No," said Tatsuno. "Did you?"

"Oh, yes, he wouldn't have gone without me," said the tipsy samurai. "Strange business out there. Not supposed to say anything 'bout it."

"Went to the shrine, did you?" asked Tatsuno.

"O-Miwa," the man said with a nod. Then he stopped and gave Tatsuno an ugly look. "I said we're not supposed to talk about that."

"Oh, I forgot," said Tatsuno. "I apologize. Will you let me buy you a cup of sake?"

The man nodded. "We were just going inside," he said.

But his two companions stopped him. "He's forgotten," one of them said to Tatsuno. "We're just leaving."

"Another time," said Tatsuno.

"What was that all about?" asked Seikei after they had entered the inn. They sat on mats that faced a long, low table where a woman was serving food.

"The new Lord Inaba—the son of the dead man—made a trip to the O-Miwa Shrine," said Tatsuno. "What does that tell you?"

"That's the place where the papermaker said the butterfly came from," Seikei said.

Tatsuno nodded. He caught the eye of the woman behind the counter, pointed to a kettle of noodle soup and then to some wriggling shrimp in a large bowl. She nodded and looked at Seikei, who asked for the same thing.

In a flash, two steaming bowls of soup with shrimp were set before them. Seikei stirred his with chopsticks to let the shrimp cook, but Tatsuno immediately raised his bowl to his mouth and sloshed in some noodles and shrimp. He bit the shrimp heads off and spat them onto the table.

While they ate, Seikei thought about the shrine that the samurai had mentioned. The same one the butterfly came from . . . but what was the connection?

After Seikei finished his soup, he asked Tatsuno, "Do you think Lord Inaba went to the O-Miwa Shrine to buy a paper butterfly?"

"What use would he have for a paper butterfly?" Tatsuno asked.

"Well . . . perhaps he was the one who left it next to his father's body."

"For what purpose?"

"I don't know. You told me it was meant to drive off evil kami. That sounds like something a person who loved his father would do. Why would the *killer* want to do that?"

Tatsuno tilted his bowl to drain the last of the soup into his mouth. "Because the ninja is a person close to the kami," he said.

This so annoyed Seikei that he was provoked into being rude. "It seems to me that ninjas are just criminals," he said.

Tatsuno looked at his empty bowl as if considering whether to order another. Then he turned to Seikei. "Perhaps that is because you have never had to suffer injustices or had your land taken, or your daughter kidnapped and no one would raise a hand to help you . . . except a ninja."

"That's not true!" Seikei said. "I am helping those people, and I'm not a ninja."

The retort drew a smile from Tatsuno. Seikei couldn't remember him smiling before. "Well, then," he said, "let us finish our business as quickly as possible. I take it you still want to deliver that list of complaints to the new Lord Inaba?"

"Yes," said Seikei, getting to his feet. "And then you'll

107

see how an honorable samurai lord acts. When he learns of the suffering of those who depend on him, he will take action."

"I'm sure he will," said Tatsuno.

They made their way through the crowded streets toward the castle. It occurred to Seikei that the people of the city showed a lack of respect for their recently deceased daimyo. There was no sign of the mourning period that should have been observed for forty-nine days after his death. Street entertainers—jugglers, acrobats, musicians, and wrestlers—were performing for the passing crowds. Even those who wore the swords of samurai were laughing, talking loudly, and playing games such as Go or *utagai*.

At the castle, Seikei and Tatsuno had no trouble entering. They passed through a gate in the stone wall that surrounded the grounds, and then over a bridge that spanned a moat, without a challenge from the guards. Apparently Tatsuno's outfit was enough to convince the guards that he had come on business.

The castle itself was impressive. It rose seven stories high, with many crested roofs jutting out over different parts of the building. High above, Seikei spotted observation posts where guards watched those who came and went. The shogun's castle in Edo was the only one Seikei had seen that was larger than this.

Getting to see Lord Inaba was more difficult than

entering the castle. Inside, they encountered a chamberlain. A gray-haired man who looked as if he had been sitting there since the castle was built, he asked what their business was.

For once Tatsuno was silent. He looked at Seikei with a raised eyebrow. "I . . . I have a message for Lord Inaba," Seikei said. "An *important* message."

The chamberlain held out his hand. "Leave it with me," he said.

Seikei shook his head. "No," he said. "I can only deliver it to Lord Inaba personally."

The chamberlain gave him a withering look. "Who do you think you are?" he said. "Lord Inaba is a busy man. He has no time to listen to the babblings of every small boy who comes to the castle." He turned to Tatsuno. "Why did you bring him in here, anyway?"

Tatsuno shrugged. "He can tell you what he told me, if he likes."

The chamberlain looked back at Seikei. "Well?" he said. "I'm a busy man too."

Seikei took a deep breath. "I am the son of Judge Ooka, an official representative of the shogun. I have been sent here to investigate conditions in Etchu Province. I wish to report my findings to Lord Inaba."

The chamberlain stared at him for a moment, then exchanged glances with Tatsuno. Tatsuno said nothing. Fine help *you* are, Seikei thought.

Finally the chamberlain said, "All right, come with

me. But if you're lying, I'll make sure you regret it deeply."

Motioning for Seikei to follow, he started up a flight of stairs. As Seikei trailed behind, he looked back over his shoulder. Tatsuno was nowhere to be seen. Either he had gone back through the entrance, or he'd become invisible, Seikei thought. No matter. Seikei was determined to keep his promise to the farmers.

14 —
WAITING FOR THE
EXECUTIONER

Lord Inaba didn't keep them waiting long. He didn't seem *that* busy, nor did he appear to be in mourning for his father. He was in fact playing a game of Go with a samurai retainer, while a geisha plucked a *samisen.* The room was a bright one at the very top of the castle. Seikei caught a glimpse of the view from one of the windows. From here, one could see all the way to the edge of the city and even the fields beyond. It was a view designed by a poet, Seikei thought. Then he realized that it was also designed to give the master of the castle warning when his enemies were approaching.

The chamberlain stood waiting silently as Lord Inaba pondered his next move in the game. Finally sliding one of the white disks onto an adjacent square, the young lord picked up a black disk and looked up. He glanced over Seikei with mild curiosity and then said to the chamberlain, "Why are you disturbing my concentration?"

The chamberlain bowed. "Lord, this boy claims to be the son of Judge Ooka, with a message for you."

"Oh?" The daimyo's eyebrows rose. "You were with Ooka in my father's castle in Edo, weren't you? Well, did he discover who the assassin is?"

"No," Seikei replied. "Or at least I don't think so."

"Then why are you bothering me?"

Seikei swallowed. "I have a petition from some of the farmers within your domain."

Seikei became aware that not only the young lord but also the samurai across the Go board and the chamberlain were all staring at him.

"Your lordship, I did not know," said the chamberlain.

Lord Inaba waved a hand to silence him. He looked at Seikei and said, "Show me this petition."

Their reaction made Seikei nervous. Too late, he started to consider Tatsuno's warnings. He pressed his lips together in determination. "First," he said, "I would like to know whether you are aware they have to pay taxes even though their crops have failed."

Lord Inaba turned to the samurai across the game board. "Take the petition from him," he said.

Seikei struggled, but the samurai was much stronger. Unfortunately, Seikei had not stored the petition inside the writing-kit drawer. The samurai took the sheets of paper from Seikei's kimono, tossing Seikei to the floor.

Lord Inaba scanned the papers quickly. "This appears to be a list of names and complaints," he said quietly. "All of it in the same handwriting. Cannot these peasants even write their own names?"

"*I* wrote them down as they gave them to me," Seikei said.

"That was kind of you. Why did you do that?"

Seikei wanted to think of a good answer. "Because I saw how they were suffering. I wanted to help them."

"I assume that Judge Ooka must have sent you here for that purpose."

"No, not exactly," said Seikei, deciding that the judge might not want his real purpose known.

"He sent you here to spy on me, didn't he?"

"Oh, no!" Seikei said. "He doesn't even know I came here to your castle."

Lord Inaba looked at the chamberlain. "How did this boy gain entrance to the castle?"

"A samurai brought him, Lord."

"One of *my* samurai? Do you know his name?"

"No, Lord. He was not familiar to me."

"Find it out," Lord Inaba snapped. He returned his gaze to Seikei. "I want to know if it's true that no one knows this boy is within my control. In the meantime, put him in the dungeon. Don't harm him—yet."

Seikei started to protest. "You cannot do this! I am here on business for Judge Ooka!"

"Silence!" roared Lord Inaba. "I am the master here now!" He handed the list of names to the samurai he had been playing Go with. "I have a simple task for you.

Find the rebellious traitors whose names are on this list and kill them."

Seikei had made the mistake of resisting again. This time his reward had been a hard knock on the head. When he awoke, he found himself lying on a cold stone floor with a headache. The place he was in was pitch dark. It was impossible to see farther than his hand in front of his face. The only light came through a grating high above. So he was startled when a voice came out of the darkness.

"Awake already? They must not have hurt you too badly."

"Badly enough," said Seikei, feeling his head and finding a lump the size of a pigeon's egg behind his ear. As he checked over the rest of his body, he found that his wooden sword was gone too.

With a shock, he remembered Lord Inaba's instructions to the samurai. "How long have I been here?" Seikei asked.

"Oh, not too long," said the voice, which sounded as if it belonged to an old man. "They've only let down one basket of food since you came, so it's less than a day. I ate your portion. I hope you don't mind. I thought it might spoil."

"I've got to get out of here," said Seikei. He had to warn Dr. Genko and the farmers that Lord Inaba was going to kill them.

Seikei heard a sound like a seagull's cry, and then realized that the man in the cell was laughing. "Don't be in such a hurry," he told Seikei. "No one bothers with you here as long as you're quiet. And they give you food, which is more than you might have on the outside. People are starving, you know."

"I know," said Seikei. "I brought a list of complaints from a group of farmers to Lord Inaba."

"And you're still alive? My, he must have something special in store for you. Maybe a crucifixion. You know, the way they execute Kirishitans and leave their bodies on the crossed sticks on the highway as a warning to others."

"He wouldn't dare execute me," said Seikei.

More seagulls' cries, a little louder this time. Seikei thought about what he'd said to Lord Inaba. It had been foolish to let him know that no one knew Seikei had come to the castle.

Someone did know, however: Tatsuno. If he told the judge where Seikei was, then the judge would arrive to free him. But the judge had told them to meet him at the governor's house in Yamato Province. That was far away; it would take Tatsuno days to get there.

If he cared enough to go at all. Tatsuno seemed to be trustworthy only as long as somebody kept an eye on him. And even then, he was likely to come up with a lie.

But if Tatsuno doesn't save me, Seikei thought, who will? Seikei would have to find a way out by himself.

"How often do they bring food?" he asked the voice in the darkness.

"Twice a day. Or at least I *think* it's twice a day. The light at the grating above dims for a while, and I suppose that's because it's nighttime."

"Who brings the food?"

"Don't bother yourself with all these questions," the man said. "They'll only take you out of here to execute you. If they were going to torture you, they would have done it already. They must not need any information from you."

Yes, thought Seikei bitterly. I brought it to them voluntarily without being tortured.

"What about you?" asked Seikei. "Are they going to execute you?"

"I think they've forgotten about me. The last person who was here—before you—said that Lord Inaba had died. Is that true?"

"Yes. He was killed in his castle in Edo."

"What a shame. Who would have done such a thing?"

"How can you say that when you're waiting here to be executed?" asked Seikei. "What did you do to deserve that?"

"I was hired to build a wall on one of Lord Inaba's estates. I did a poor job, and it fell down."

"For that you're going to be executed?"

"Well, I deserved it, didn't I?"

"I think it's a very cruel punishment for a minor offense," said Seikei.

"That's what my wife said. She was going to appeal to Lord Inaba for mercy. He was such a kind man, you see."

Seikei's head began to hurt even more. "That makes no sense," he said. "I spoke to some farmers in the southern part of Lord Inaba's domain. They told me that Lord Inaba took their stored rice for taxes, even though they hadn't been able to grow anything in two years. Now they and their families are starving."

"Oh, yes," said the man. "That's true all over the province."

"Then how can you say Lord Inaba was a kind man?"

"Why, because he knew nothing about the people's suffering. If he had, he would have taken steps to ease it."

Seikei was exasperated. He could hardly believe the man's stupidity. "Of course he knows—or knew. It's his domain."

"No, the chamberlain is the one who's in charge of enforcing order," the man said. "And it was Lord Inaba's son who gave the order to collect taxes from the farmers, even when they couldn't pay." He sighed. "I guess the son is the new lord. That means as soon as someone remembers about me—"

"How do you know this?" Seikei demanded.

"Working on the wall, I heard things," said the man.

117

"One day I heard Lord Inaba's son and the chamberlain talking. They were worried that Lord Inaba himself would find out what they were doing."

"Why didn't you tell—"

"Shh, shh," the man whispered. "Listen."

They heard footsteps high above them, near the grating.

"The guards are bringing food," said the man. "Either that or—" He didn't finish, but Seikei knew what he meant. Either that or they were coming to execute someone.

15 ~
On the
Nightingale Floor

The grating slid back and two faces peered down at the prisoners. Seikei didn't recognize either one of them. "Hai!" one of them shouted. "Old man! Did the boy wake up yet?"

"No," said the man in the cell with Seikei.

"Don't lie," said the other guard from above, "or we'll throw some rats down there to keep you company."

"I'm awake," said Seikei, not wanting to get the old man in trouble.

"We're lowering a rope," said the second guard. "Tie it around your waist."

A coil of rope came tumbling over the side of the grating.

"If they burn you to death," whispered the old man, "it's better to breathe in the flames at once so you'll die quickly."

"I'll come back and get you out of here," Seikei responded. He could hear the old man scuttle off into a corner, getting as far away from Seikei as he could. Seikei understood why. No one liked being in the presence of a madman, because such a person had been invaded by evil kami.

Seikei wound the rope around himself. He tied a slipknot at the end, so that he could release himself quickly when he was out of the cell.

The two guards were careful, however. While one of them pulled Seikei up, the other took a few steps back, waiting with his hand on the hilt of his sword.

As soon as Seikei reached the top, he started to loosen the rope. But the samurai who had pulled him up said, "None of that" and quickly bound Seikei's hands behind his back.

"This way," said the other samurai, heading down a corridor. Leading Seikei on the end of the rope like a dog, the second guard followed.

"I am here on official business for Judge Ooka," Seikei said. "It is your duty to release me."

Neither man paid any attention. The one who was leading the way turned into another, darker corridor, and Seikei heard a strange sound—a muffled blow, as if someone had struck the wall with a gloved fist.

The samurai who held the rope heard it too. He called out, "Chigo?"

Almost too quickly for Seikei to realize what was happening, a third samurai emerged from the dark corridor. He leaped at the second guard and wrapped one arm around his neck. Seikei heard a sickening crack, and the guard fell to the floor like a stone.

The new samurai turned, and Seikei could see his face in the shadows. "Tatsuno!" he said.

Tatsuno clapped his hand across Seikei's mouth. "No sounds," he whispered. "Do what I tell you . . . nothing else."

Seikei nodded. Tatsuno seemed to have become a different person. His body was tense, as full of energy as a bow drawn and ready to shoot an arrow. His wary eyes blazed with determination as he untied the rope that bound Seikei's hands. Instead of discarding it, he coiled it around his forearm and motioned for Seikei to follow.

They went down a corridor that was lit only by a smoky torch made of pine resin. Beyond the torch appeared to be nothing but empty blackness. Tatsuno went that way, stopped, and then felt along the stone wall to his right. Finding something that Seikei could not see, Tatsuno gave a push and the wall swung inward.

He stepped through the opening and Seikei followed. As he entered, he stubbed his toe and nearly tripped. He hadn't seen the flight of stairs here leading upward. Seikei looked up to see Tatsuno a few steps higher, glaring down at him. "Should I carry you?" he hissed. "Or can you walk without sounding like a blacksmith forging a sword?"

Seikei thought he hadn't been *that* noisy, but he made an extra effort. The steps seemed to go on forever, and he concentrated so much on putting one foot silently above the other that he lost track of where he was. Without meaning to, he bumped into Tatsuno, who had stopped at the top.

The colder air here was enough to tell Seikei that they were nearly outside the castle. He poked his head past Tatsuno and saw that they stood on a rampart that ran around the second story of the castle. It was covered by an overhanging roof, but the stone wall on the opposite side had slots in it where archers could fire on enemies below.

Tatsuno put out a hand to keep Seikei back on the staircase. Slowly he uncoiled the rope, tied a loop in one end, and threw it toward something Seikei could not see. Whatever it was, the rope caught it. Tatsuno pulled back gingerly and the rope became taut. He tied the end nearest him to an iron dolphin that had been set into the stone parapet for decoration.

Tatsuno motioned Seikei forward. "I am going to use the rope to pull myself along the length of the wall to the observation tower at the corner. Inside there will be a window. Watch me and then follow. Do *not* put your foot on the wooden floor of the rampart. Understand?"

Seikei nodded. "Nightingale floor," he whispered. He remembered the one at Lord Inaba's castle in Edo.

This one was nearly as wide. Seikei could have leaped across it only with a running start.

Tatsuno leaned over and grasped the rope. Swinging himself through the air, he cleared the floor and put his feet on the wall. Step by step he started moving down the rope toward the corner of the castle.

Seikei took a deep breath and followed suit. After he had the rope in his hands, it wasn't as difficult as it looked to swing his feet across. Balancing on the wall was tricky though. He had to move his hands to the left on the rope, then his feet sideways on the wall, repeating the movement over and over. He was moving too slowly; Tatsuno would reach the corner long before he did.

But in his rush to catch up, one of Seikei's hands slipped. Without thinking, he put his left foot down to steady himself.

The floor sang.

As the first board moved under Seikei's foot, it touched a second one. The friction between them caused a loud squeal. The second board rubbed against a third, and the squealing went on and on until Seikei thought it must soon wake everyone in the castle.

Down at the far end of the parapet, a guard popped out of the observation tower and saw them. With a shout, he rushed toward Tatsuno, drawing his long sword as he did so.

Tatsuno sprang down from the wall and took a

fighting stance. Seikei gasped, for it appeared that Tatsuno meant to face the samurai's razor-sharp sword with nothing but his bare hands.

But then Tatsuno took something from his kimono. It was small enough for his hand to conceal what it was. With a swift movement of his arm, as if cracking a whip, Tatsuno threw it in the direction of the samurai.

Seikei heard a noise like the whir of hummingbird wings, but saw only a golden flash of light. Then the samurai screamed, dropped his sword, and put his hands to his face.

Tatsuno turned and yelled at Seikei: "Forget the floor! Run! Follow me!"

Seikei jumped down and ran. All the boards were singing now, and the samurai guard was on his knees, blood pouring from between his fingers. Seikei dodged him but then heard more shouts from behind him.

He didn't turn to look, because Tatsuno was already inside the guardhouse. By the time Seikei reached it, a few seconds later, Tatsuno was kneeling on the window ledge. "Jump," he said, pointing.

Seikei drew back. "But we're too high above—"

He didn't finish, because Tatsuno had grabbed a handful of Seikei's kimono and lifted him as easily as if he were a baby. With one smooth motion, he tossed Seikei out the window.

For a moment, Seikei was paralyzed. He was falling into a yawning blackness that seemed to have no bottom. Then he saw the moon below him and realized it was a reflection on water. He was going to land in the moat.

An odd thought popped into his head: This is the way I felt in the village. Once more I'm about to step into the moon.

His fall broke with a splash and he was carried underwater. Struggling to swim to the surface, he feared that he would not find it. But once again the sight of the moon led him to safety. Only then, after he drew in great lungfuls of air, did he realize that the moat stank of garbage and sewage from the castle's privies.

Another splash sounded nearby. It was Tatsuno, who urged Seikei to swim for the other side. High above, there were shouts now from more than one guardhouse. Something flew by Seikei's head, making a noise like a bee. Then another. The second time, he saw it break the surface of the water: an arrow.

Seikei hadn't known he could swim that fast. He reached the opposite side of the moat after only a few hard strokes. The muddy bank was slippery, but Tatsuno had climbed it before him. Seikei reached for his outstretched hand.

Just as Tatsuno pulled Seikei onto solid ground, Seikei heard him grunt. Looking over, Seikei saw an arrow sticking from Tatsuno's shoulder.

Tatsuno ignored it, pushing Seikei forward. "Run before the gate closes," he said.

Seikei didn't need any further urging. He found himself moving forward without thinking. Keeping his eyes straight ahead, he saw the moon through the open gate. Behind him he heard footsteps. He hoped that was Tatsuno, but didn't dare to look.

From the wall above the gate, Seikei heard a shout and saw the flash of a lantern. He heard a grinding noise—the rumble of wooden gears. The gate was closing.

He made himself run faster, hurtling forward so that he was on the verge of falling. The open space between the gate and the ground shrank with each step he took. At what seemed like the very last moment, he leaped through, ducking his head under the falling gate.

He wanted to stop. His body was crying out for air, but Tatsuno caught hold of him and pushed him on-ward. "Just a little farther," he said. "I have horses."

16 —
THE NINJA'S STORY

By the time Seikei and Tatsuno mounted their horses, they could hear the gate of the castle reopening. Lord Inaba's men were ready to pursue the escaped prisoner and his accomplice.

Tatsuno led the way into the narrow streets of the town. The hoofbeats of their horses sounded loud, echoing against the silent, sleeping houses and shops. There must be night patrols, thought Seikei, just as in Edo, where any movement after nightfall would arouse suspicion and alarm.

Then they heard another sound: their pursuers, with many horses, drawing closer.

Tatsuno reined his mount to a halt and slipped off its back. The arrow was still lodged in his shoulder, Seikei saw. The point had gone clean through and out the other side. Blood was flowing from the wound. It must be weakening him.

"Take your horse in there," Tatsuno said. He gestured toward a dark alleyway between two shops. It was a good hiding place; Seikei would never have noticed it if Tatsuno had not pointed it out. He dismounted and led his horse into the narrow passage.

Tatsuno slapped his own horse on the rump and threw its reins across its back. The frightened animal ran off as Tatsuno stepped into the alley. "Lord Inaba's men will follow it," he said.

They led the other horse deeper into the shadows. Seikei was confident no one could see them from the street. But Tatsuno stumbled, falling against Seikei, who reached out to steady him.

"You're badly hurt," said Seikei. He thought of Dr. Genko, who unfortunately was at least a day's ride away.

Tatsuno sank slowly to the ground. Seikei could hear him breathing hard, and realized with a shock that he might die. "Thank you for saving me," Seikei said. The words sounded strange. Seikei did not dare to add, "I wanted to thank you before it was too late."

Tatsuno made a wheezing sound. Seikei could not tell if he were laughing or preparing to die. "Neither of us is safe yet," Tatsuno said. "Listen."

They froze as a troop of mounted samurai rode past their hiding place. Seikei stroked his horse, trying to calm it.

"When they find the other horse, they will return," said Tatsuno. "We've got to move on."

"You're not strong enough," Seikei said. "We've got to find a doctor."

"I have my own medicine," Tatsuno replied. "Come here and help me."

"What do you want me to do?"

"Take hold of the end of the arrow and break it off."

"Break it off?"

"Yes. I can't pull the arrow out if the head is still on."

Seikei took a deep breath to steady himself. "All right," he said.

It was awkward. He had to grasp both ends of the arrow, and every time it moved, it caused more blood to flow from Tatsuno's shoulder.

The shaft of the arrow was strong. Seikei felt the point dig into his hand as he strained to break it off. He knew this must be hurting Tatsuno, but the ninja made no sound. Finally, with a splintering snap, the arrow cracked.

Tatsuno immediately reached for the other end and drew it from his shoulder. Still, he did not cry out or even grunt. Seikei was amazed at his self-control.

Yet the effort left Tatsuno exhausted. "Inside my belt," he told Seikei, "is a pouch with healing herbs. Bring it out for me."

Seikei did so. Inside the leather pouch he found sweet-smelling moss that had been sprinkled with dried leaves and seeds.

"Place some of it on both sides of the wound," said Tatsuno.

Seikei was surprised to find that the moist moss clung to Tatsuno's shoulder as if it were growing at the base of a tree. Tatsuno pulled his kimono back into place and tied his belt. He tried to stand up, but couldn't.

Seikei said, "You should rest. I will awaken you if I hear the samurai returning."

Tatsuno nodded.

But Tatsuno was the one who woke Seikei, who had not been able to keep his eyes open. Seikei sat up with a start. He had been dreaming that the samurai whose horse they had taken was coming down the alley with his swords drawn. Just as Seikei was about to cry out, Tatsuno had covered his mouth.

He blinked and looked at Tatsuno. "How did you know what I was dreaming?" Seikei asked.

Tatsuno smiled. "Your face told me," he said. "You have not yet learned the secret of hiding your true feelings."

Seikei stared at him. Tatsuno seemed to have recovered. He looked refreshed. "You look much better yourself," Seikei said. "How is your shoulder?"

"I am ignoring it," Tatsuno replied. "And you were quite helpful. It would have been difficult for me to break the shaft by myself."

"It was my fault that you were shot in the first place," said Seikei.

"Not at all," replied Tatsuno. "We all make our own choices. If I was foolish enough to try to rescue you from Lord Inaba, I should accept the consequences."

"Lord Inaba!" Seikei exclaimed. "I forgot. Lord Inaba intends to send samurai to kill Dr. Genko and the farmers. We have to warn them!"

Tatsuno shook his head. "If Lord Inaba intends to harm them, we cannot save them."

"But . . . if they know Lord Inaba's men are coming, they could hide or run."

"Run? Where? Most of them have never left that village in their lives. How would they live? What would their families do?"

"Even so—" Seikei began, but Tatsuno cut him off.

"Enough. Let us go now. There are people in the streets already. The shops are opening. We must lose ourselves in the crowds."

They found some empty sacks in the alley and threw them over the back of the horse. Tatsuno undid the topknot that was the mark of a samurai and carried a sack to hide the Inaba insignia on his kosode. He hid the two swords underneath his clothing. To a casual onlooker, they might pass for farmers heading home after selling their goods in the city.

Twice, they passed samurai who were scanning the passersby carefully. Seikei nearly froze, but Tatsuno growled, "Keep your head down." The samurai did not stop them.

Finally they reached the outskirts of the city. Ahead lay the road that led back to the fork where one branch would take them west, and the other one, south.

"I want to ask you something," said Seikei.

"If you don't mind, I'll ride the horse for a while," said Tatsuno.

"Of course," Seikei replied. He was surprised. Perhaps Tatsuno's wound pained him more than he let on. In fact, he even allowed Seikei to help him onto the horse's back.

When he was comfortably seated, Tatsuno said, "You wanted to ask me something?"

"Yes," said Seikei. "What was that you threw at the guard when we were trying to escape from the castle?"

"It was a *shuriken*," Tatsuno told him. "A thin metal disk with sharp teeth. Very useful for discouraging anyone in your way."

"Do you have more of them?"

Tatsuno gave him a look. "Why do you ask?"

"Why . . . I thought we might meet others who were in our way."

"They are a ninja's weapon, not a samurai's. And besides, a ninja never reveals how many weapons he has."

"You really *are* a ninja, aren't you?"

"Your father told you I was. Didn't you believe him?"

Seikei's face reddened. "Of course I did. You just didn't—"

"Seem like one? That is one way of being invisible."

Seikei nodded. "Tell me something else. Why would a ninja want to kill Lord Inaba?"

Tatsuno didn't answer right away. Seikei looked up to see if he had fallen asleep on the horse.

When Tatsuno finally spoke, his voice was low, as if he were telling the story from a great distance. "At first ninjas were people who lived in the mountains, where they grew very close to the kami of nature. But then shoguns and even the emperors were uneasy that people could live beyond their control. So they sent samurai to conquer us."

Tatsuno paused, and Seikei thought about what he meant by saying *us*. No one had ever told him about ninjas from their side.

"By that time," continued Tatsuno, "the ninjas had grown so close to the kami that we were able to confuse the samurai and drive them off."

"How did you confuse them?" asked Seikei.

"To know that," Tatsuno said, "you would have to be a ninja."

"Well . . . what happened to the samurai then?"

"They left, they died . . ." Tatsuno waved his hand. "Who knows? But after that, the ninjas knew the shogun might send more samurai. So we developed our skills further. Only now we concentrated on skills that would help us defend ourselves."

Tatsuno paused again, staring into the distance, thinking about the past. "We became the best killers

133

anyone had ever known," he said finally. "Better than any samurai." There was a note of pride in his voice, but deep sadness as well.

His voice changed. "So do you know what happened then?" he asked Seikei.

"They frightened people," Seikei replied.

Tatsuno gave a little laugh, sharp as a cough. "That's true. And the shogun and daimyos, who were, in those times, often at war with each other, came to value us. Because we were so skilled at going where others could not, and killing when others could not. So whenever the shogun and the daimyos—and anyone else— wanted a killer, they knew that they should hire a ninja."

Tatsuno grew silent again, riding the horse slowly while Seikei walked alongside. "Do you remember your question?" Tatsuno asked quietly.

Seikei had nearly forgotten. "Why would a ninja want to kill Lord Inaba?" he asked once more.

"Because someone paid him to do it," Tatsuno answered.

"The farmers?" asked Seikei. "Do you think the farmers did it?"

"It is clear," said Tatsuno, "that Lord Inaba—both the old one and the new one—had many enemies."

17 —
THE BUTTERFLY SOARS

The sound of approaching hoofbeats interrupted their conversation. Realizing that it must be more of Lord Inaba's samurai, Tatsuno urged his horse into a copse of trees near the road. Seikei ran after him.

Tatsuno slid off the horse, his knees buckling as he reached the ground. It was clear that although he didn't complain, he was still weak from his wound. "Find a tree and hide behind it," he told Seikei.

"What about you?" Seikei asked. "They'll see the horse."

"I will make certain they don't," said Tatsuno.

Seikei found a tree whose trunk was broad enough to conceal him. He ducked behind it, but couldn't resist taking a cautious look as the samurai approached.

They were coming from the south. There were twenty or more mounted warriors, covered with armor made of leather strips bound together. Most were also wearing war helmets, carved into ferocious figures designed to frighten enemies.

Seikei shivered. There were no enemies for Lord

Inaba's men to conquer down that road—except some humble farmers armed only with sticks and tools, whose only crime had been to want their families to live.

Seikei looked over at the place where he had left Tatsuno. He was astonished to see that there was no sign of either him or the horse. Seikei turned and looked all around, but the ninja and the horse had entirely vanished.

That was just as well, for the samurai would surely have seen him. And although Seikei could only see the samurai from a distance, it looked to him as if one of them was the man whose horse Tatsuno had taken.

A flash of light shone briefly from the front line of the riders. Seikei had to shield his eyes. As the glare vanished, he saw one of the riders toss something to the ground.

When they had passed by, disappearing around the next bend in the road, Seikei cautiously stepped from behind the tree. He looked around again. Still no trace of Tatsuno. In fact, the silence in the grove of trees seemed strangely overwhelming. It was as if a cold wind had come through and blown away all sound. Seikei tried to shout, but found that his throat was closed from fear.

He ran toward the road, preferring the risk of being seen to remaining any longer in the dark, silent forest.

Just as he stepped into the hoofprints left in the snowy road by the samurais' horses, he saw the flash of light again. This time it came from the road. Seikei went over and picked up the object that the samurai had thrown away.

He recognized it. It was the wire frame that held the two crystals Dr. Genko had looked through to examine Seikei's foot. But the crystals were broken now. Only a few jagged pieces of them were left in the wire frame, which was twisted and ruined.

"Do you understand what that means?"

Seikei whirled at the sound of the voice. It was Tatsuno, still leading the horse.

"Where did you come from?" Seikei asked in a shaky voice. The ninja's sudden appearance had frightened him.

"I was in the woods," Tatsuno replied, "but I was invisible. That doesn't matter. What do you think the object in your hands means?"

Seikei bit his lip. "That those samurai have been to the village where Dr. Genko lives. We must go and see if we can help them."

"It must be obvious even to you that we are too late," said Tatsuno. "We must go meet your father now."

"It may *not* be too late," said Seikei. "Those people trusted us. We *have* to do something to help them."

"Become a warlord and come back to kill Lord

137

Inaba," said Tatsuno. "As long as you believe in dreams."

Seikei was angry. "I could hire a ninja to help me. If there were any brave ones around."

"And if you had enough money," said Tatsuno. "Ninjas are not as brave as they are clever."

"You mean greedy," said Seikei.

Tatsuno shrugged, mounted the horse, and headed south along the road. Seikei followed. A cold wind blew flakes of snow at their backs. When they came to the fork in the road, Tatsuno turned and asked, "Do you still have that paper butterfly?"

"Yes," Seikei replied.

"Give it to me."

Seikei hesitated. "What are you going to do?"

"Come on, you don't need it any longer. We know where it came from."

Reluctantly Seikei took it from his kimono. To tell the truth, he was glad to be rid of the blood-stained thing. He handed it to Tatsuno.

Tatsuno spread the butterfly's wings as wide as they would go. He held it high in the air, resting it on his palm. A gust of wind captured it and blew it toward the south, toward the village where Dr. Genko lived. Straining his eyes in that direction, Seikei thought he saw wisps of smoke in the sky.

"That is the best we can do for them," said Tatsuno.

He turned and headed west. Seikei watched the butterfly, thinking that it must soon fall to the ground. But, carried by the wind, it went on until it was out of sight.

Tatsuno was right, Seikei admitted to himself. There was nothing else he could do. Not now at least. But he would make sure Lord Inaba was punished for this.

The road was bleak and empty of everything but snow. They passed a few farmhouses that seemed to be deserted. Their inhabitants had given up, starved to death, or perhaps gone to try to make a living in a city.

Seikei and Tatsuno stopped at one of the farmhouses for the night. They had no way to build a fire, for the coals in the hearth had long ago burned out. There was nothing to eat, for either them or the horse. After the sun set, the snow started to fall harder. Tatsuno led the horse inside to shelter it. Seikei realized the house was actually a little warmer with the horse, even if it smelled.

Seikei still had the writing kit, but it was too dark to write anything. As he lay restlessly on the floor, he tried to think of a poem. Basho had often consoled himself that way when he encountered unexpected hardships.

But every time Seikei started a poem, it seemed to describe how it felt to sleep with a horse. Had Basho ever done that?

Fortunately, the next morning they had not traveled far before finding a farmhouse that was occupied. At first, it didn't seem so lucky. Seeing smoke coming from the chimney, Tatsuno and Seikei approached the house. But a farmer and his son—about the same age as Seikei—emerged. The older man carried an ax; his son, a pitchfork.

"They think we're bandits," said Tatsuno. "They have so little to preserve that they guard it fiercely." He stepped forward, holding his hands out to show them he meant no harm. Seikei knew by now that Tatsuno's hands were as dangerous as any weapon—and of course with one of his deadly little shuriken, he could have caused either the man or boy to drop to his knees, screaming.

Instead he offered them the horse. In return he asked only for two bowls of rice.

The farmer was very suspicious. He examined the horse closely, starting with the teeth. Then he checked its legs and hooves.

Seikei thought the man was an idiot. If Seikei had had two bowls of rice, he would have traded Tatsuno for the horse himself, just so he could ride the rest of the way.

Finally the farmer agreed to the deal. Even then, he wouldn't allow Tatsuno and Seikei to enter the house, fearing some trick. His son went inside and emerged with two bowls of warm rice—not even particularly generous bowls, Seikei noticed. Although he was glad to eat what there was.

When they had finished their meal and set out on the road again, Seikei asked, "Why did you make such a poor bargain?"

"You didn't think having a full stomach was worth a horse?" asked Tatsuno.

"A horse is certainly worth more than two bowls of rice," replied Seikei.

"Perhaps not, when you're hungry and have no way to eat the horse," replied Tatsuno. "Besides, the horse was hungry too. We had nothing to feed him. If he had died, it would have been our responsibility. It was I who took him from a comfortable stable and out of the city. He carried me on his back all day without complaining. I would have been very cruel and ungrateful to let him starve."

Seikei admitted this was so.

"And besides," said Tatsuno, "it's very difficult to make a horse invisible."

They continued on the road for several days, stopping overnight at shrines or monasteries whenever they could, sleeping in caves when no other shelter could be found. Turning south, they passed Lake Biwa, where the water along the shore was frozen.

Seikei had never seen the vast lake before. "I want to stay here until I think of a poem that will do justice to it," he told Tatsuno.

"No poem ever will," Tatsuno replied, "because a great and wonderful kami dwells here. How can you put into words the grandeur of the kami—even a small kami in a stone or a drop of water?"

"In a poem, you don't try to completely describe it," said Seikei. "What you must do is recall a small part of it, and the rest follows."

Tatsuno shrugged. "Then you can remember a small part, and write it down later. Come on—your father will wonder what has kept us all this time."

"He's probably solved the case by now and found the killer," said Seikei. "But I still want to report Lord Inaba's behavior to him."

"Why do you think he's solved the case?" asked Tatsuno.

"I thought that as soon as we left the old paper-maker," said Seikei. "He told us that the paper for the butterfly came from O-Miwa Shrine, remember?"

"Yes."

"And O-Miwa Shrine is in Yamato Province."

"That's right."

"Which is where we're going anyway because the judge told us to meet him there."

"So you think—"

"Somehow he knew all along that the murderer

would be there. And he's had days to capture him. The case will be solved by the time we arrive."

"I doubt that," said Tatsuno. "I doubt that very much."

He sounded very sure, Seikei thought. There was only one way he could be so sure, but that . . . that was impossible.

18 —
A PARTING

They approached the city of Nara from the north. Soon after entering the outskirts, Seikei saw a mammoth wooden structure that towered above all the other buildings.

Tatsuno noticed him staring at it, and said, "That's the Great Buddha Hall of Todai-ji. Shall we pay it a visit?"

Even though Seikei was eager to report to the judge, his curiosity overcame him. When they reached the temple, he and Tatsuno removed their sandals, leaving them with dozens of other pairs on the steps.

Though the building was immense, it was nearly as light inside as out. Thousands of candles were burning, set in holders on the walls all the way up to the ceiling. They illuminated a gigantic golden statue of the Buddha that towered over the worshippers who stood in front of it.

Joining the crowd, Seikei and Tatsuno were gradually swept toward the statue like leaves floating in a stream. The closer they got, the larger the statue seemed to become. Finally, at the very base of it, Seikei bent his head back as far as he could, trying to see the Buddha's face. From here, all that was visible was his nose.

"People say," remarked Tatsuno, "that a bandit once hid in the left nostril of the statue for two years, coming out at night to eat food that people had left as offerings."

"Is that all you can think of in such a holy place?" asked Seikei.

"I thought it was an interesting story," Tatsuno retorted. "Not a bad place to hide, if one needed a hiding place."

"Do *you* need one?" Seikei asked.

"No one is looking for me," said Tatsuno.

Perhaps they should be, thought Seikei.

Outside again, Seikei saw that the city streets were filled with Buddhist monks and nuns, as well as Shinto priests. "This is the opposite of Edo," he said, "where half the people you see are samurai."

"There are countless temples and shrines in the city," Tatsuno told him, "many of them hundreds of years old. They are all that remain from the days when this was the capital of Japan."

"Where is the O-Miwa Shrine?"

"That's not here," said Tatsuno. "It's a day's ride to the south."

"I am eager to see it," said Seikei.

"Don't you remember what the papermaker told you?" asked Tatsuno. "You shouldn't go there."

"But if the judge has not solved the case," said Seikei, "then I must."

"If you do, stay off the mountain."

"Why?"

"Because that is where you will find the murderer."

Seikei laughed. He couldn't help himself. "Then that is what I *must* do."

Tatsuno shook his head. "You think you are brave, but really you are foolhardy. There are times to attack and times to save your own life."

"Everyone must die in time," said Seikei, "so one should prefer honor over life."

Tatsuno grunted. "That sounds as if it came from a book," he said.

"It did," admitted Seikei, "but that does not make it any the less true."

Tatsuno reached into his kimono and took out a small black object. He handed it to Seikei, who saw that it was a stone. Holding it closer, he saw that veins of green ran through the rough black surface. "What's this?" he asked.

"Something to take with you if you are foolish enough to go onto the mountain," said Tatsuno.

Seikei turned it over in his hand. It was about the

size of a duck's egg. It seemed like an ordinary stone, except for its unusual color.

"I have no idea why," said Tatsuno, "but I have decided your life is worth saving."

"How will this save my life?" asked Seikei.

Instead of answering, Tatsuno pointed to a large house just down the street. "That's the governor's mansion," he said. "Your father will be there."

Seikei excitedly ran toward it. All of a sudden, however, he realized he didn't hear Tatsuno's footsteps following. He turned to see why not.

Tatsuno was gone. A group of monks in yellow robes walked past the spot where he had been, tolling prayers on their rosary beads. A farmer unloaded an oxcart full of melons. Two boys ran by with a dog.

Otherwise the street was empty. Seikei put the stone into his kimono and walked toward the governor's mansion.

Two samurai guards stood at the mansion's front door. They eyed Seikei disapprovingly as he approached. He realized how he must look. He picked a piece of straw off his sleeve. It was still clinging there from the stable they'd slept in last night.

He bowed in front of the guards. "I am Ooka, Seikei," he said formally, "the son of Judge Ooka Tadesuke, who I believe is a guest here."

The guards looked at each other. "We were told to

expect you," one of them said to Seikei, "but your . . . perhaps you would like a bath first. The public bath-house is in the next street."

"I met with a few mishaps on my journey," Seikei explained. "But I must report to the judge as soon as possible."

The two samurai shrugged and stood aside for Seikei to enter. One pointed to a hallway that led to the back of the house. "You'll find them in the garden," he said.

As Seikei approached, he heard laughter. Emerging from the doorway, he was struck by the sight of a beautiful stone garden, with raked gravel punctuated by a series of large stones. The stones had obviously been chosen with great care to appear natural and ordinary. An irregular-shaped pool with goldfish swimming in it was at the far end of the garden. There, sitting under a *gingko* tree, feeding the fish, sat two men who looked almost like twins.

One of them saw Seikei and beckoned him to come closer. It was the judge, looking pleased.

Amazingly, the governor (for that must be the other man, Seikei realized) was even fatter than the judge. The two of them looked as if they might never leave this spot, but instead turn into rocks that would become part of the harmonious garden.

"Ichiro, here is my son Seikei at last," said the judge. "Seikei, this is the honorable governor of Yamato Province, my friend Kamura Ichiro."

Governor Kamura nodded his head gravely. Seikei bowed in return.

"Would you like something to drink?" said the governor. "Plum wine? Sake? They'll warm you up."

Seikei was actually quite hungry and would have preferred rice and hot tea, but it was impolite to say so. He realized that both the governor and the judge had been drinking for some time, even though it was early in the afternoon.

The judge's powers of observation were not dulled, however. He passed a plate of *sushi* to Seikei and said, "These are quite delicious. The only reason we haven't finished them is that we're trying to relive our youth and can only find it in bottles."

The governor spoke up with a smile. "We were members of the Six Immortals of the Wine Cup, your father and I," he said.

"Well, we needn't go into the details of that as long as Seikei is here," the judge said hastily. In a different voice, he added, "I hope I don't have to remind you, Ichiro, what his arrival means."

The governor waved a hand good-naturedly. "Indeed, Tadesuke, you have won the wager," he said. "I should have known that anyone you chose as a son would let no obstacle stand in his way."

While they were talking, Seikei had been eating sushi, trying not to finish the entire plate of them too quickly. But he was so surprised at what he heard that he said, "You mean you didn't think I would arrive here? Why not?"

"Well," said the governor, "the fact that your father sent you with a ninja as your guide . . ." Instead of finishing the sentence, he rolled his eyes.

"I warned Tatsuno to watch out for Seikei, and I think he knew I was serious," said the judge.

The governor shook his head. "You can't trust any of them," he said. "They'll steal the pillow from under your head if they catch you sleeping."

"He saved my life," said Seikei.

The governor was so surprised, he nearly spilled his wine. "You must be mistaken. Is he waiting outside for a reward?"

"No, he disappeared," said Seikei.

"A trick of theirs," the governor murmured.

"That reminds me," said Seikei, turning to the judge. "Throughout our journey, Tatsuno showed that he could escape from almost any danger. How was it that you were able to catch him back in Edo?"

The judge smiled. "I have a few tricks of my own," he said. "When you chased him through the alley, I knew he wouldn't be expecting to meet me at the other end."

"That's the only way to catch a ninja," the governor explained. "Take him by surprise."

"And are you ready to do that now?" the judge asked Seikei.

"Do what?" Seikei responded.

"Catch another ninja."

Seikei must have shown his befuddlement, because the governor added, "That's why your father and I have had such a nice reunion these past few days. He came here as soon as he realized that the ninja who killed Lord Inaba must be at the O-Miwa Shrine."

"Then you *did* know that all along," Seikei said to the judge.

"Yes," the judge replied. "You probably noticed that Tatsuno understood that too."

"But then . . . why did you send me to the papermaker in Shinano? And to Lord Inaba's domain?"

"Well, as to the papermaker . . . it never hurts to check for proof of my conclusions. I can be wrong, you know."

"I doubt it," said Seikei.

"The papermaker *did* confirm my suspicion, then?" asked the judge.

"Yes, he said the paper was made for the O-Miwa Shrine. He also told me not to go there."

"Sound advice," remarked the governor.

"I had other reasons for sending you on that journey," said the judge. "I wanted you to learn more about ninjas. Did you observe Tatsuno closely?"

"Yes," said Seikei.

"What did you conclude?"

"That he is a great deal more skillful than he appears to be," said Seikei.

"A good lesson," said the judge. "You said he saved your life. I hope you told him you were grateful."

"Well . . . I did express my thanks."

"Did he tell you about the fox?"

"He said only that the killer was a ninja named the fox. But I . . ." Seikei hesitated.

"Yes?"

"I began to think that Tatsuno himself was the killer."

The judge considered this. "No," he said, "I believe the killer had already gone to O-Miwa Shrine by the time we met Tatsuno."

Seikei was taken aback. He seldom questioned the judge's reasoning, but this conclusion puzzled him.

"Well," Seikei asked the judge, "if you already knew where the murderer was, why did you want us to find out who Lord Inaba's enemies were?"

"Didn't I explain that?" asked the judge. "I thought it must be obvious."

"Even *I* can see that," said the governor.

"You see," the judge told Seikei, "the true murderer is the person who paid the ninja to kill Lord Inaba. That is the person we want to find."

"But the ninja—"

"Is only a servant," finished the judge. "It would be as if we had found the blade that cut Lord Inaba's throat and said that was the murderer."

Seikei sat down on a mat, trying to take all this in.

"And so," said the judge, "I sent you to discover who

might have hated Lord Inaba enough to want to hire a ninja to kill him. Did you find anyone like that? Someone who might have reason to want Lord Inaba dead?"

Seikei looked the judge in the eye. "Yes. Many people," he said. "I should start with myself."

"More wine," the governor called to a servant.

19 —
AT THE SHRINE

By the time Seikei finished telling the story, it was late afternoon. He had left nothing out, admitting his own stupidity in telling Lord Inaba that no one knew where he was. The governor and Judge Ooka had listened raptly, commenting only a few times.

The governor shook his head in disapproval when Seikei described how he met with the farmers to hear their complaints. "It is their duty," said the governor, "to obey their lord, even if his actions seem harsh. He may have a motive we do not know about."

Before Seikei could reply, the judge spoke up: "But the lord has a duty to protect and preserve his people. What are they to do if he fails in his duty? In the past, some angry farmers have formed small armies and fought the samurai. Appealing to Lord Inaba with a petition seems quite reasonable to me."

"One thing leads to another," said the governor grumpily.

However, when Seikei told of being imprisoned by

Lord Inaba, the governor growled. But his anger turned to laughter and applause when Seikei related how he had escaped. The judge was less demonstrative, but Seikei saw from his face that Lord Inaba would someday pay for his treatment of Seikei.

But Seikei wanted more than that. When he had finished the story, he said, "I suppose Dr. Genko and the rest must be dead." He looked at the judge and governor, hoping they would disagree. But the governor nodded slowly. "It seems likely," he said. "Of course some may have escaped if the samurai were not diligent in their duty."

"Lord Inaba must be punished for that," said Seikei.

The governor coughed and looked away. The judge spoke softly: "I'm afraid no one can punish him for that. He has the right to rule his domain however he wishes."

"But that's . . . that's unfair," said Seikei.

"It is the shogun's command," the judge replied.

Seikei sat in miserable silence, regretting everything he had done.

Finally the governor said, "You probably accomplished what you set out to do. Take pride in that."

"What do you mean?" asked Seikei.

"Well, these farmers—or some group like them—no doubt hired the ninja who killed old Lord Inaba, wouldn't you say? So if they were punished for one thing instead of another, what's the difference?"

"No," Seikei said firmly. "They couldn't have hired the ninja. They were too poor. And so were all the other people in Lord Inaba's domain."

"How about that doctor you mentioned?" asked the governor. "He could have put away some money over the years."

Seikei shook his head. He wanted to think of some way to excuse himself so he wouldn't have to listen to the governor any longer.

The judge spoke up. "You told us that you were an enemy of Lord Inaba."

Seikei looked at him. "Yes," he said. "Do you think that was wrong of me?"

"No," replied the judge, "but I suspect you have let your anger confuse you."

Seikei blinked. The judge's advice was always correct, so Seikei must have missed something. It was true, he was angry at Lord Inaba. He wanted revenge, and it was also true that such a desire could affect one's judgment. He must calm himself and think.

"You have done well," the judge told him. "Take a bath and sleep soundly tonight. Remember that by completing your journey you have helped me win a wager with the governor."

"Oh, you're not going ahead with that, are you?" said the governor.

"Of course I am," replied the judge. "It is very clear

now that the path will lead us to the O-Miwa Shrine. And you promised me your permission to visit the mountain if Seikei arrived here safely."

"Those priests," the governor protested. "You know they don't want anyone on that mountain of theirs. They will complain to me; they will send letters to the shogun."

"Someone else is already on the mountain," said the judge. "We must find him. Surely the priests will not protect a killer."

"They will if he's a ninja," said the governor.

The next morning, Seikei felt considerably better. He'd slept a long time and when he awoke had a breakfast nearly as good as the ones at Judge Ooka's house. Someone had taken his old kimono and replaced it with a handsome fresh one that had the governor's crest on it. Next to the new kimono were the contents of Seikei's old one—a few coins, Dr. Genko's eye frames, the black-and-green stone Tatsuno had given him, and the writing kit.

Seikei felt a pang of sorrow at seeing the eye frames, and once more vowed silently to avenge those who had trusted him. Picking up the stone, he cradled it in his hand, wondering why Tatsuno had given it to him. It felt warm—strange for a stone—as if it held something alive. Of course it was said that every object in nature had a kami within, but this kami must be very active. Seikei slipped it inside his new kimono.

Finally he looked at the writing kit. Seikei saw that only one of the thin, finely made sheets of rice paper remained, and he resolved to use it to write a poem worthy of the gift. That, however, would have to wait.

The governor appeared as Seikei was finishing breakfast and presented him with a marvelous gift: a pair of swords. Real ones. Nothing had been said the previous day about Seikei's losing his wooden sword at Lord Inaba's castle. It was a disgrace, but because he'd defended himself until being knocked unconscious, it was excusable.

Seikei bowed low, thanking the governor. "You are worthy of them," the governor said. "I hope you keep them . . . a long time."

"I will always keep them," said Seikei.

The governor looked a little distracted as he bade the judge and Seikei farewell. "Better if I don't go with you," he said. "You understand, Tadesuke."

"We will return soon," promised the judge.

The governor had also provided Seikei with a fine horse to ride, and the judge still had the trusty steed that was used to carrying his weight. "The governor was very generous to give me these swords," said Seikei.

"They once belonged to me," said the judge.

"Really?" said Seikei. "Then I am doubly honored."

"Long ago, he won them from me in a wager," said the judge.

"And now you have won them back?"

"No, he was just being sentimental. He thinks you'll be killed."

Seikei was too shocked to respond at first. Then he cleared his throat and asked carefully, "Why does he think that?"

"Because you completed the task I set for you. That won for me the prize in our latest wager: his permission to go onto Miwayama, the mountain at the O-Miwa Shrine."

"Yes," said Seikei. "To catch the ninja who murdered Lord Inaba."

"Oh, no, we could never catch him there. He is far too powerful there."

"But you caught Tatsuno before."

"This ninja and Tatsuno are not one and the same," the judge cautioned. "And even if they were, the ninja will draw power from the mountain."

"How?"

"Tatsuno didn't tell you? This is a sacred mountain. The shrine, unlike other shrines, has no dwelling place for its guardian kami. The mountain itself is its dwelling."

159

"Yes, he did tell me," said Seikei. "I remember now." Tatsuno had also told him things about the ninjas drawing close to nature. Seikei wished he had listened a little more carefully.

"You'll see when we reach the shrine," said the judge.

The journey took them most of the day, even on horseback. When they finally reached it, they saw that the priests at the shrine were preparing for the New Year's festival. Banners were fluttering from poles to welcome the *toshikami,* the divine spirits of the incoming year. A *simenawa,* or sacred rope, hung across the top of the torii gate that marked the entrance to the shrine. From it dangled strings of folded-paper figures. Seikei recognized them: butterflies.

People from nearby villages had already arrived to bring gifts of food and drink for the kami of the shrine. Each person who could afford it wore a new kimono. After leaving their offerings at the sanctuary, the people would stay to watch the dancing, plays, and festive ceremonies that were part of the New Year festival.

The shrine itself seemed small to Seikei. Surrounding the main building were several lesser structures where priests and travelers ate and slept. But the main building itself looked oddly shortened, for although it had the usual place for people to pray and to leave their offerings, it ended where the most sacred part should have been. At that point, at the base of the mountain, there was only another simenawa rope stretched between two wooden poles.

Beyond was woodland—groves of pines that grew denser as they gradually rose to the clouds. A gray-green mist wafted down from the summit, which was impossible to see from the shrine itself. The cone-shaped mountain was not a high one, but Seikei felt chilled at the sight of it. There was a forbidding spirit about it, something that said people should not go there.

A young priest came to meet Seikei and the judge after they had left their horses at the shrine's stable. He wore a high black mushroom-shaped cap and was dressed in a long brown kimono with sleeves that were so full, they reached nearly to his knees. "The governor sent a messenger yesterday to tell us you were coming," he said. "I am sorry we cannot welcome you as Your Honor deserves, for the festival is taking up so much of our time."

"We understand," said the judge. "Really, all we need is a place to spend the night before we go onto the mountain tomorrow."

The priest shook his head. "No one is permitted to climb the mountain beyond the edge of the shrine," he said.

"Yet some do go there," the judge replied. "I believe someone is on the mountain at this moment."

"If that is true," said the young priest carefully, "he has received the permission of the *kannushi,* the head of the shrine."

"Then we must obtain his permission too," said the judge.

20 —
THE KANNUSHI SPEAKS

They waited two days before they were admitted into the kannushi's presence. Seikei was astonished that anyone would dare insult an official of the shogun so flagrantly. If the judge wished, he could call on the governor to send samurai warriors to enforce his orders.

Nor did Seikei understand the judge's reaction. He acted as if he'd come to the shrine to take part in the weeklong New Year's festivities. He and Seikei spent their time with the people of the village watching the plays and dances that were part of the celebration. Along with everyone else, the judge partook of the sticky-rice patties called *moshi-moshi*. He even took a turn swinging the wooden mallet used to pound the rice before it was formed into patties.

Seikei admitted that the taste of the moshi-moshi reminded him of the ones he had enjoyed as a child. During the New Year, even his father the merchant had relaxed. Once, Seikei recalled, Father had actually danced in public at their local shrine.

But those days were in his childhood. Now he had to

think of serious matters. After the long journey that had led Seikei to this place, he was eager to finish the task. He would not be able to return to Edo with the judge until the person who hired Lord Inaba's murderer had been discovered. And with the murderer himself on the mountain overlooking the shrine, Seikei found the delay in chasing him almost impossible to bear.

"What if he escapes?" Seikei asked the judge on the morning of their second day of waiting.

"Who? Oh, the ninja?" replied the judge. "He won't leave the mountain while we're here. I told you—that's the source of his power."

"Do you think he is too powerful for us to defeat him?"

"I think that is what the kannushi must be trying to decide," said the judge.

"And what will you do if he decides not to let us go onto the mountain?" asked Seikei.

"Let us see what he says first," the judge replied.

The next morning, the young priest told them, "You are to be honored. The kannushi will admit you to his presence after morning prayers."

"Thank you," said the judge. After the priest left, the judge said to Seikei, "Clearly the kannushi has made up his mind."

"What do you think his decision will be?" asked Seikei.

"I think it will be a wise one," replied the judge. "The shrine would not have survived so long if its kannushis had not made wise decisions."

After the prayers, the judge and Seikei remained in the shrine's prayer hall as others in attendance left. The young priest led them to a small room to one side of the hall.

Inside, seated on a mat with a teacup in front of him, was an old man dressed the same as the young priest, except that his garments looked as if he'd been wearing them for many years. The closer Seikei approached, the older the man seemed to be. His skin was dry and thin, like an old manuscript that was flaking away. His skull was bare, and his face so emaciated that Seikei thought that he must not have eaten anything for years.

The young priest motioned for Seikei and the judge to sit. As they did, the kannushi raised his eyes to them. Seikei saw that although the life force had drained from the rest of his body, the eyes were still keenly alive. They were like the last two glowing coals in a fire that had almost gone out.

Yet they could still burn if they touched you, Scikei discovered. After glancing briefly at the judge, the kannushi focused on Seikei. His eyes seemed to bore right to Seikei's inner spirit. Seikei knew that he was being examined.

"Why have you come here?" The kannushi's voice

was sharp and shrill, like a cricket's chirp. Surprisingly, he directed his question to Seikei. Seikei looked at the judge.

"I am Ooka, an official of the shogun's government," the judge told the kannushi. "We are searching for a ninja who murdered Lord Inaba while the daimyo was in Edo under the protection of the shogun."

"Why do you think this ninja is here?" the kannushi asked.

"Because he left a red butterfly made of paper that was sold to your shrine. And because it is well known that ninjas regard Miwayama as a place of sanctuary."

"They have good reason," said the kannushi. "The kami of the mountain is their protector."

"And you permit them to enter the shrine's holiest place."

The kannushi nodded. "The ninjas are generous with their offerings, and the mountain kami accepts them."

"If the kami accepts the ninjas," said the judge, "then it will accept us."

"You are samurai," said the kannushi. "You bring your swords here. There can be no death on the mountain. The kami will not tolerate it."

"This ninja has brought death elsewhere," said the judge, "and yet he returned to the mountain."

"He has purified himself," said the kannushi. At last Seikei understood why the ninja had left the red butterfly next to Lord Inaba's body. That was his *own* act of purification. He had to dispel the evil kami that surrounded death so that he would be able to return to the mountain.

The kannushi turned his eyes on Seikei again. "You did not answer my question," he said.

Seikei was flustered, trying to remember the question. "I . . . I came here because I wish to see justice done," he said, "and because the path my father set for me has led me to this place."

Wrinkles appeared briefly at the corners of the kannushi's eyes as if he wanted to smile but had forgotten how. "You have brought something with you," the kannushi said. "Show it to me."

Seikei thought he meant the butterfly. Would the judge be angry to learn that it had been lost? "I don't have it anymore," said Seikei. "It was needed to purify another place where death had been."

"You are mistaken," the kannushi said. "Show me what you have inside your garment."

Seikei brought forth the writing kit, the coins, Dr. Genko's wire frames, and then touched the stone Tatsuno had given him. It seemed even warmer now.

That was what the kannushi was looking for. His eyes shone with a kind of reverence as Seikei displayed it. "Where did you get that?" the kannushi asked.

"Someone gave it to me," said Seikei.

"You have a generous friend," said the kannushi.

167

"This is a *gofu,* a powerful one that may protect you if your heart is pure." He looked at the judge. "Does he have a pure heart?"

"I believe so," said the judge.

The kannushi returned his gaze to Seikei. "You may go onto the mountain," he said. Then he added, "Alone."

"You do not have to do this," said the judge as he and Seikei walked to the simenawa rope at the base of the mountain. "I am not at all sure that I should allow you to go. There is no way I can protect you there."

Seikei turned to look at him. "Father," he said, "the first time you assigned me to follow a path, you sent Bunzo in disguise to watch over me. And the second time you trusted me to follow a path, you yourself rescued me when my life was in danger. Even on the journey I have just taken, you told Tatsuno not to let me come to harm."

Seikei took a deep breath. "But, Father," he continued, "I want to be worthy of being your son, the son of a samurai. I can only do that by facing danger, by being willing to lose my own life if necessary. I can never do that if you are always waiting to protect me. Because then it is only like boys playing at war, pretending.

"And, as Basho once wrote, 'Even if I should die on the road, this would be the will of Heaven.' "

The judge smiled. "I often think of those words of

Basho's when I am about to leave on a journey, but I am much older than you." He sighed. "I am afraid I chose too well when I asked the shogun to let me take you as a son."

Seikei felt his heart in his mouth. Did the judge regret choosing Seikei? "Why do you say too well?" asked Seikei.

"Because I thought I would be sure to have a son to observe the proper ceremonies for me for the required forty-nine days after my death. Instead I have a son who is willing to lay down his own life in pursuit of honor."

"Father," said Seikei, "I pledge that I will do my best to return and someday say the prayers for your spirit."

The judge nodded and smiled. "I see it would be useless for me to forbid you to go onto the mountain," he said. "Was it Tatsuno who gave you that stone?"

"Yes," Seikei said.

"Did he tell you why?"

"No," said Seikei. "He only said that he'd decided my life was worth saving."

The judge smiled. "I see that I was not wrong to trust Tatsuno. Remember one thing: You do not need to capture or kill the ninja. You need only find out who sent him to kill Lord Inaba."

"I will carry out the task you have set for me," said Seikei.

They had reached the dividing place, where a simenawa rope strung between two wooden posts separated the world of humans from the world of the kami. Red paper butterflies hung from the rope, their wings fluttering in the wind as if they were struggling to free themselves. One of the strings that held the butterflies was empty, and Seikei knew that was where the one that was later found in Lord Inaba's chamber had hung.

The young priest accompanied Seikei and the judge. He offered Seikei a pail of water and a dipper. "You must purify yourself," he explained. Seikei knew the ritual from watching at other Shinto shrines. He took a mouthful of the water, which had a salty-sweet taste. He swirled it around and then spat it onto the ground. Finally he rinsed his hands in the water.

"I am ready," he said. The judge's face was grimmer than Seikei had ever seen it, but Seikei lifted the rope and crossed to the other side.

21 —
ON MIWAYAMA

Seikei walked only a few steps before entering a thick stand of trees. When he paused to look back, he saw the judge just once. After that the forest closed in, and Seikei was alone.

It was difficult for him to make any progress up the mountain. There was no trail, of course, because people seldom set foot there. The ground sloped steeply upward, and it was covered with snow that concealed branches, logs, and rocks. Earlier Seikei had put on thick *tabi* socks and a new pair of bamboo sandals, but his feet sank into the snow above his ankles. Eventually, the tabi became soaked and the cold air started to freeze them.

Seikei stopped. He was breathing hard from the effort, and could see his breath in the air like puffs of smoke. He wasn't sure how he was supposed to find the ninja. Somehow, Seikei had expected that once someone invaded his domain, the ninja would appear.

"Hai!" Seikei called out. "Ninja! Tatsuno!" He still

suspected that Tatsuno might have been the killer all along, even though the judge thought otherwise.

There was no answer. The mountain was silent, even though Seikei knew there must be many living things here.

Seikei reached into his kimono for the black-and-green stone. It was still warm. As he cupped it in his hands, he felt its warmth spread through him. The kami within the stone was giving him help of some kind, Seikei thought.

He decided it was time to call the kami of the mountain, to appeal to it.

Everyone in Japan knew how to do that. On entering the torii gate of a shrine, they clapped their hands. Seikei did so now. He made as much noise as he could.

"Kami!" he shouted. "I appeal to you, spirit of this mountain! Show me the ninja! I must speak with him. I promise not to pollute your holy dwelling. Tell me! Give me an answer." Around and around he turned, facing all parts of the mountain. "Kami! Hear me!"

The sun moved slightly then. A sliver of light shone through a gap in the treetops. Seikei looked toward the place where the sunlight touched the ground.

A deer stood there. Apparently it had been hunting for food. Under the snow there were still shoots of grass that were nourishing. Now it was looking at Seikei. Seikei waved his arms, but the deer didn't move.

It was a doe, not a large one, and seemed gentle.

But it kept on looking at him, so long that it began to make Seikei nervous. "Hai!" he shouted, waving his arms again.

Still the deer stared at him. Seikei walked toward it, and the deer dug at the snow with its front hooves. It gave Seikei a final look, tossed its head, and walked off slowly.

Seikei made his way to the spot where the deer had been standing. He saw footprints in the snow. Some, the deer had made, but there were others as well. Seikei bent low and examined them.

They were made by a fox. Seikei remembered the fox prints outside Lord Inaba's castle, where the killer had escaped. And the guards' dreams. A chill went through him. It was one thing to chase a man, even a ninja—but to capture a man who was at times a fox . . .

The tracks led farther up the mountain, and after a moment Seikei began to follow them. It was not easy, even though the ground was covered with snow. In open places, the sun had melted some of the snow and the trail was washed out. Seikei had to circle these spots to find where it began again.

He also had to keep reminding himself to take his eyes off the tracks every so often and look up. He remembered the story his mother had once told him about a hunter who followed bear tracks and walked right into the bear's mouth.

Seikei knew that was only a story, but he also realized

that somewhere, the tracks would end. He wanted to be well prepared before he reached that spot.

It was a longer journey than he expected. The tracks didn't lead directly upward. They wound back and forth as if the person who made them wanted to avoid being followed. Twice the trail even doubled back and crossed itself. That gave Seikei a great deal of trouble sorting out the older tracks from the fresh ones.

Finally, however, he looked up and saw where the trail ended. It was a cave, not far from the summit of the mountain.

Seikei approached it warily, knowing that from within the deep black opening someone could be watching him.

He reached the entrance without drawing any response. Staring inside, he saw only that the cave headed down into the heart of the mountain.

Deciding he would prefer fighting out in the open, he shouted, "Ninja! Come out and face me!"

The only response he got was an echo—and a faint one at that. Seikei realized that his voice sounded reedy and weak. He reached inside his kimono again, grasping the stone to give himself strength.

Should he wait here for the ninja to emerge? He had to come out sometime, didn't he?

Unless the cave had another exit.

Seikei thought about his promise to return so that one day he could say the mourning prayers for the judge. No doubt the wisest course would be to wait here for a while. If nothing happened, Seikei could return to the judge and report that he had followed the path as far as he could.

But not to the end.

Basho's words again ran through Seikei's head. If a man saves his own life by being a coward, Seikei thought, then what is the value of his life? Heaven has granted me the wish that once seemed an impossible dream: to be a samurai. I must prove myself worthy of that.

He put his hand on the hilt of the sword and stepped into the cave.

The tunnel led downward toward the heart of the mountain. After Seikei had taken only a few steps, the light from the tunnel's mouth no longer lit the path in front of him. He took each step more carefully than the last. Pausing between steps, he stopped to listen. In the absolute silence of the cave, it should be easy to hear any sound. However, his own breathing drowned out any other noise. He forced himself to be calm, using a meditation technique Basho had taught him.

After another few steps, he slowly became aware of another sound. At first it seemed like buzzing, as if there were a hive of bees sheltered here from the cold. After listening for a while, however, Seikei decided that the sound rose, fell, stopped, and then rose again. It was like the pounding of waves at the seashore.

Or like snoring.

Yes, thought Seikei, that was what it must be! The ninja was not far away, lying asleep in the cave, snoring. He must feel very safe.

Seikei considered what to do. With a drawn sword, he could rush forward and kill the ninja before he woke up, whether he was a fox or a man.

However, then Seikei would not find out who hired the ninja to kill Lord Inaba. According to the judge, that was more important.

And if the ninja really was Tatsuno . . . Seikei didn't like to admit it, but he would feel sad to have to kill Tatsuno.

"Hai!" he shouted, more out of frustration with himself than for any other reason.

The snoring stopped. In fact, now there was no sound at all, for the ninja had been able to stop breathing entirely. He must have great powers of self-discipline. But Seikei knew he was just a few steps up ahead in the darkness.

Listening.

22 —
THE FOX'S CONFESSION

Seikei stood absolutely still for so long that his knees began to ache. Yet it was the ninja who moved first. Seikei heard the soft rustle of silk—and suddenly realized what that sound meant.

He dropped to the floor of the cave just in time to hear the sound of hummingbird wings overhead. Only Seikei knew it was not a hummingbird: it was a razor-sharp shuriken, thrown right at the spot where Seikei's face had been an instant before.

Scrambling on all fours, Seikei struggled to climb back up toward the mouth of the cave. He heard the ninja start to pursue him. Realizing he couldn't escape, Seikei rolled over on his back and drew his sword partway from its scabbard, ready to use it.

The ninja heard the sound and halted. He did not know exactly where Seikei was, but he knew that if he rushed forward in the darkness, he might run right onto the point of a blade.

"Who are you?" the ninja said.

The voice was not Tatsuno's.

Seikei was afraid to reply, for the location of his voice would tell the ninja where to direct the next deadly shuriken.

Slowly Seikei inched backward along the rocky floor, keeping his sword pointed toward the darkness that hid the ninja.

Another shuriken whizzed overhead. This time Seikei heard the chink of the metal disk as it struck the wall of the cave.

He stopped to think. If he tried to get back to the mouth of the cave, the ninja only had to follow him. There, Seikei would make a perfect target, for then he would be outlined against the light coming from the entrance.

Seikei's hand slipped. He had put it down on a loose rock. That gave him the idea for a desperate solution. It was better, he decided, than waiting for the ninja to zero in on Seikei with his shuriken.

Raising himself into a crouched position, Seikei drew his arm back and threw the rock into the center of the darkness. As he turned and ran, he heard a surprised grunt that told him the rock had found its mark.

Seikei ran as fast as he could, his feet wobbling against the stones underfoot. In a few steps he spied the cave entrance and hunched his back, making himself into as small a target as possible. Closer and closer he came, telling himself to go on without fear.

Then he was directly in the entranceway—and still no whirring sound overhead. He came through it with a bound and headed for a large rock nearby. Using it for shelter, he crouched down, turning back to watch the cave entrance. The ninja emerged slowly, aware that now he too could be a target. Seikei was relieved to see that he had the form of a man. He was somewhat older than Tatsuno, but moved with the grace and stealth of a fox. He wore a black kimono, like the ninjas of myth and legend, but even from here Seikei could see that the ends of the sleeves were frayed and the cloth was faded in places.

The ninja looked around, the way an animal does when entering a clearing. Seikei saw his eyes. They were yellow, the only part of him that did not appear completely human. "Who are you?" the ninja called. "What have you come here for?"

Seikei wondered if he should answer. The ninja's hands were empty, but Seikei had no doubt he could reach into his kimono and launch another shuriken if he knew where Seikei was.

Still, why else had Seikei come if not to question the ninja? Seikei was in as safe a position as he would ever be.

"I am Ooka, Seikei," he shouted. "I have come to question you about the murder of Lord Inaba."

The ninja laughed. When his mouth opened, Seikei saw that several of his teeth were missing. "Is that so?"

the ninja said with a touch of mockery. He had heard Seikei's voice, and recognized that it was not yet that of a man.

"Come, show yourself," the ninja said, coaxing now. "I will not harm you."

"You tried to harm me in the cave," said Seikei.

"I was merely defending myself," the ninja replied smoothly. "You startled me."

"I could have done more than startle you if I'd wished," Seikei told him.

The ninja thought this over. "Yes, that's true," he said. "You had a sword, and you found me asleep. I should be more cautious, but people seldom disturb my rest. How is it that you were allowed on the mountain?"

Seikei was tired of answering questions. "You have not yet told me *your* name," he said.

The ninja smiled. "My name is Kitsune."

"That isn't a name," said Seikei. "It means 'fox.' "

"A man takes the name that suits him," the ninja replied with a smile that made Seikei clasp the hilt of his sword even more tightly. "Why have you come to question me about Lord Inaba's death?"

"Because I think you murdered him," said Seikei.

"Really? What makes you think so?" asked Kitsune.

"Because you left a red paper butterfly there," Seikei said. Kitsune did not reply, so Seikei continued. "And the man who made the paper told me that it had been purchased by the O-Miwa Shrine. The priests here allow you to make the mountain a haven because you are generous to them." Now Kitsune's lips were stretched into a thin line.

"And I even saw the empty place on the string on the simenawa at the base of the mountain, that you took the butterfly from," Seikei said.

Kitsune remained silent a moment longer and then said, "If you know all that, then why did you not execute me in the cave?"

Seikei hesitated. "Because I thought you might be Tatsuno," he said.

"Tatsuno?" the ninja said with scorn. "Tatsuno is a disgrace, a failure, a . . . a . . . I would not walk on the same side of the street as Tatsuno."

"I saw him act bravely," said Seikei. "He saved my life."

"How much did you pay him?" Kitsune asked.

"Nothing," Seikei replied.

Kitsune threw up his hands. "You see?" he cried. "What kind of ninja is that? And to think he's my brother."

"Your brother?" Seikei was stunned, but then on a second look, he saw the resemblance between the two.

"Yes," said Kitsune. "I admit it, but only to you, because you'll never be able to tell anyone." He put one hand inside his kimono again. Keeping it there, he began to walk toward the rock where Seikei was hiding. "You know what?" said Kitsune. "I think you didn't kill me in the cave because you were afraid to. Have you *ever* killed anyone?"

"I . . . I almost did," said Seikei. "Once."

"Ah," said Kitsune, "a shame you didn't kill *me* when you had the chance. Now you'll never know what it feels like." He continued walking, slowly but deliberately.

"Stay back," Seikei warned, in a voice that he hoped sounded threatening. Then he realized his dilemma. His weapon, the sword, could defeat Kitsune, but only if Seikei stood up and exposed himself to the ninja's weapon. Seikei would be cut down by one of the deadly spinning shuriken before he could use his sword.

Unless he could find something else to throw. Seikei looked around him. If there were any loose rocks, they were covered by snow.

Then he realized he had a rock right inside his kimono. He looked up. Kitsune was still approaching, but in no hurry. He was far enough away to give Seikei time.

Seikei stood and pulled out the black-and-green stone. As he drew his arm back to throw it, he saw a look of surprise replace the ninja's confident smile.

"Stop!" shouted Kitsune. "Where did you get that?"

Seikei kept his arm in throwing position, wondering if this was a trick. "Why?" he asked.

"You're not supposed to have that. Only a ninja may possess one of those."

"What is it?"

Kitsune's face changed again. He was calculating now, plotting. "It's nothing," he said. "Merely a pretty rock. Don't throw it. Why don't you just give it to me and I'll let you go?"

Though Seikei would have been relieved to do that, he forced himself to say, "I didn't come here for that. I came to find out who hired you to kill Lord Inaba."

"Aha." Kitsune nodded. "And if I tell you that, it will be an admission of my guilt. Very clever."

"We already know you are the killer."

"We?" Kitsune looked around. "Don't tell me there are more of you. That gofu will only work for the person carrying it."

"I'm speaking of my father, Judge Ooka. He sent me to find out who hired you."

"Judge Ooka? Hmph. That explains why Tatsuno was so friendly to you. The judge proved him innocent once."

"Tatsuno?"

"Yes. Of course it was only by accident that he was innocent. He intended to steal something, but someone else got there before him. Tatsuno was charged with the crime anyway, just because he was a ninja."

A look of sudden understanding came over Kitsune's

face. "And of course it was *Tatsuno* who gave you the gofu, wasn't it?"

Seikei was silent. He wished Tatsuno had told him more about the purpose of the stone.

"All right," said Kitsune. "The gofu really belongs to me, you know. Tatsuno stole it. So you should, by right, return my stolen property."

"I don't believe you," said Seikei. "If you claim this stone is your property, then come down and report it to Judge Ooka."

"Well, of course he won't believe me either."

"Then tell me the name of the person who hired you, and I'll give you the stone."

Kitsune thought for a moment. "The same objection applies there. Go back and report any name you please."

"I cannot do that," Seikei said. He thought of the writing kit. "Here," he said. He let go of his sword and took the kit from his kimono. "Use this to write the name of the person who hired you. Sign it. That will be good enough."

"This would be the same as my confession," Kitsune said. "Then I could never leave the mountain."

"My father wishes only to know who hired you," Seikei said. "He will not try to punish you."

"How do I know that?" Kitsune asked.

"You have my word of honor," said Seikei.

He tossed the kit to Kitsune, who scooped up some

snow and used it on the ink stone to make ink. Kitsune took his time writing the confession. He signed his name with a flourish of the brush, as if he were an artist completing a great work of calligraphy.

Then he rolled the page up, tucked it back in its compartment, and held out the kit. "Let us exchange New Year's gifts," he said.

Seikei warily stepped from his hiding place, still holding the rock threateningly. "How do I know you will keep the bargain?" he asked.

"You don't," said Kitsune, "but if ninjas did not do what they agreed to do, they would soon be out of work. Bad for their reputations. We are as honorable as you samurai think yourselves to be."

Seikei approached the ninja. He reasoned that at close quarters, his sword would be more effective than Kitsune's shuriken. He held out the stone. It seemed very warm now. Kitsune offered the writing kit.

They were exchanged. "And now," said Kitsune, "you had better get off this mountain, for the gofu was your only protection against the kami."

Seikei needed no urging. A feeling of emptiness had overcome him as soon as he had let go of the stone. He turned and walked as swiftly as possible without breaking into a run. At first he feared that a shuriken might come whirling toward the back of his head, but eventually he realized that the ninja wasn't going to seek that kind of revenge.

Even so, the mountain seemed if anything more frightening on the way down. Once he slipped and slid into a large pine tree. He looked up to see a deer standing not far away, watching him. It looked like the same deer he'd seen earlier, but who could tell? This time, the deer seemed to view Seikei as an intruder on the mountain. He hurried on.

Seikei had the feeling that many eyes were watching him now. Creatures he could not see . . . stones, trees—all of the mountain was aware of his presence. And that he did not belong here. Time passed. How long, Seikei could not tell. On the mountain, time seemed to go more slowly.

A wave of relief washed over him when he saw the simenawa with the red butterflies hanging from it that separated the mountain from the world of humans. And there, just beyond, was the judge, waiting. Seikei was deeply touched, for it must have taken a great effort for him to stand there for so long.

Seikei slipped under the rope and bowed to show his gratitude. "Father," he said, "I have followed the path you pointed out for me."

He handed the judge the writing kit. "The murderer's confession is in here." Seikei realized he was shaking, unnerved by his trip down the moutain.

The judge took the kit, removed the paper, and unrolled it. He read its contents quickly and nodded. "Did he tell you what he wrote?" asked the judge.

"No." Seikei was suddenly afraid. Perhaps the ninja had in the end had the last laugh by writing some taunting remark.

"You accomplished not only the task I set for you, but the one you took on for yourself," said the judge. "The ninja writes that the person who paid him to kill Lord Inaba was . . . Lord Inaba's son Yutaro."

23 —
A New Year's
Celebration

Seikei slurped one of the long, long *toshikoshi* noodles from his bowl. It was a New Year tradition for the long soba, or noodles, to be served. Eating them was supposed to increase your fortune and luck in the new year.

Seikei and the judge were back in the governor's mansion. The governor had insisted that they stay for the New Year's Day celebration. Actually, he wanted to hear from Seikei the story of his adventure on the mountain. Even though Seikei had told it several times by now, the governor never got tired of it.

The judge was right, Seikei thought: The governor *didn't* think I could climb Miwayama and return alive.

The governor was, however, a man who clearly enjoyed celebrations, and for this one he set out all the food and drink anyone could want. He had appointed Seikei to be the *toshiotoko,* or "year-man." This meant Seikei had to draw the first water of the new year from the well, make tea from it, set out a special breakfast for the household, and finally, lead the offering ceremony to the toshikami—the spirits of the new year. Though it seemed like a lot of work, being toshiotoko was a great honor, and anyway the governor's cook took care of preparing the breakfast.

The governor's own children and grandchildren arrived to join in the day's festivities. Actors had been hired to disguise themselves as demons and dragons, and they kept popping up to frighten the children, who responded with squeals of laughter. Everyone knew that the real demons were kept out of the house by the simenawa that hung over the doorway. Instead of red butterflies, however, this simenawa was festooned with white strips of paper, like everybody else's.

After a while, somebody took the children outside to beat the ground with sticks and sing. This was done every New Year's Day to drive away birds that might eat the seeds farmers planted. Even though the governor had no crops to plant, the children did it anyway—just as Seikei and his brothers and sisters had, even though their father was a merchant.

The house was quieter with the children gone, and the governor poured Seikei a cup of plum wine. "There's something I want to know about your battle with the ninja," the governor said.

Seikei sighed and politely pretended to take a sip of the wine. He'd already had two cups, and even though the porcelain cups were hardly any bigger than his thumb, there was still a lot of celebrating to do. Besides, plum wine didn't taste good with the noodle soup.

"It really wasn't a battle," said Seikei.

"Oh, it was," the governor said. "To think, though—you had him in front of you asleep and could have sliced off his head right then. That sword is in good condition, you know. Razor sharp."

Seikei glanced at the judge, who winked. Even though the governor didn't understand why Seikei didn't kill the ninja, the judge did. That was all that mattered.

"I thought the most interesting part of his story was Seikei's meeting the deer," said the judge in an attempt to change the subject.

"Why is that?" asked the governor.

"I suspect that the deer was the kami of the mountain," replied the judge.

The governor glanced at Seikei. "If so, your son was fortunate. Many people say that the sight of a kami can be enough to kill a person."

"That is why it took the form of a deer," said the judge. "And besides, Seikei had something to protect himself."

"Do you mean the stone?" asked Seikei. "The one that Kitsune wanted so badly?"

The judge nodded.

"The kannushi called it a gofu," said Seikei. "What did he mean?"

"A gofu," said the judge, "is a talisman, a lucky charm, some people say. A few shrines, especially very old ones like O-Miwa, sell gofus to people who believe they have magical powers."

"Maybe if you'd kept it," said the governor with a chuckle, "you could have made yourself invisible."

Seikei thought it more likely that it had enabled him to see Kitsune as a man and not a fox. He looked at the judge. "Do *you* believe the gofu had magic powers?" he asked.

"It worked well for you," the judge said with a smile. "You said that Lord Inaba was your enemy, remember?"

"Yes."

"I was afraid you had overlooked the fact that I sent you to find the enemies of the old Lord Inaba. You returned as a foe of the new one. As you discovered—and proved with the ninja's confession—the greatest enemy of the old Lord Inaba was the man you regarded as *your* enemy, his son. I suspect the father may have learned how his son was treating the people of the domain, and was planning to disinherit him. But the son acted first."

"What will happen to him?" Seikei asked.

"The governor has already sent a message to the shogun in Edo," said the judge. "It tells what you have discovered. I added my conclusion that the current Lord Inaba is responsible for the death of his father."

191

"Will the shogun punish him?"

"Perhaps the shogun will allow the new Lord Inaba to choose an honorable way out of the situation."

Seikei knew that meant the daimyo would be compelled to kill himself rather than face public execution or disgrace. Compared to what he had done to others, it was too mild a penalty to pay.

"And Kitsune?" asked Seikei. "Do you think there should be no punishment for him?"

"Oh, I think you punished him thoroughly," said the governor. "He's not accustomed to defeat. In fact, you should watch out that his path doesn't cross yours again. Don't be fooled. He's a ruthless man."

"Is it true that Tatsuno is his brother?" Seikei asked the judge.

"Yes," the judge answered. "And equally true that I concluded Tatsuno had been falsely accused of a crime. What Kitsune did not tell you was that *he* was the person who actually committed the crime."

"He did? And he would have let his brother be punished for it?"

"He *intended* for his brother to be punished for it. That was when I learned how difficult it was to capture Kitsune. I was unable to do it."

Seikei raised his soup bowl to get the last of the broth. He found one more noodle, and as he lowered the bowl, part of it was hanging from his mouth.

"Look at that," said the governor, sounding envious.

"You got the longest noodle. That means the most good fortune will come to you this year."

"You have earned it," the judge said.

Seikei slurped the last of the noodle into his mouth. The judge's praise warmed him as much as the broth. But Seikei still remembered with sorrow those he had failed—Dr. Genko, Sada, Joji, the farmers. It had not been the will of Heaven for Seikei to die on the journey. But those others . . . he had been unable to prevent their deaths.

The judge had told him it was impossible to thwart the will of Heaven. Perhaps if Seikei had never taken down their complaints, they would not have died. But then, what would life be if we did not struggle to make ourselves better? In the new year, Seikei resolved, he would try harder to be worthy of the title of samurai. Perhaps he could begin by returning to Kanazawa and rescuing the prisoner who had spoken to him in the dungeon. . . .

"The children will be back soon," the judge said. "Why don't we have a few more moshi-moshi before they get here and eat them all?"

Author's Note

We received a letter from a girl in Wisconsin who read *The Ghost in the Tokaido Inn* while traveling in Japan. She pointed out that we had Seikei turn north to get to the shrine of Ise from the Tokaido Road, when he really should have turned *south*. So, like Seikei, we'll try to do better in the future.

In this book, we have used the names for Japanese provinces as they were in the year 1736, or as Seikei would have written, the twenty-seventh year of the reign of the Emperor Nakamikado. What was then called Yamato Province is today's Nara Province. Etchu Province is now Toyama Province, and Shinano Province is now Nagano Province.

There is an actual castle town named Kanazawa, but it was the headquarters of the Maeda family, not the imaginary Inaba family of this story. The O-Miwa Shrine does exist, more or less as we have described it, to honor the kami of Miwayama (or Mount Miwa). And no, you can't go onto the mountain even today.

According to one source we consulted, the word

origami—meaning "paper folding"—was not used until the 1880s. Previously, the term was *orikata*. However, we used *origami* because it will be more familiar to our readers.

The quotation from Basho's travel diary is adapted from the translation by Donald Keene: *The Narrow Road to Oku* (Kodansha, 1996).

As readers of *The Ghost in the Tokaido Inn* and *The Demon in the Teahouse* know, Judge Ooka was a real person whose reputation for wise and honest decisions won him promotion to high office. He served Yoshimune, the eighth shogun of the Tokugawa family, who ruled Japan between 1717 and 1744. Tales about Judge Ooka have remained popular, causing some to call him the Sherlock Holmes of Japan. This story, and the character of Seikei, came from the imagination of the authors.